# Love First, Dear Love

**Ramya Paramasivam Gupta**

ISBN
Paperback  979-8-89961-342-5
Hardcase  979-8-89906-263-6

# Contents

# Prologue

# PART 1

# Chapter 1: Source Energy

Faithful,

A loyalist

Another is the same kind

The other is a different thing from the other half or being othered,

He is my kind, my own kind

After hearing he needed me more than anyone, I took the next flight to London, though my family wouldn't have accepted this decision. Not knowing the consequences that would follow, I simply followed my heart.

The home was beaming with sunshine during one of the hottest summer days, when roads were melting like chocolate. I remembered his phrase about how my "brown skin was pouring honey during the hot, sweaty sun." I removed my flats and dipped my feet in the soothing, cold marble floor, where East met West perfectly harmoniously. My mind and heart felt a certain serenity, away from the hustle and bustle of the modern world. Deep within me, the beautiful blue clouds and delightful cold breeze provided a temporary calmness.

I made a conscious effort to keep thoughts of him at bay, not wanting my spirits to sink lower. The absolute emptiness of his absence made my heart ache. Waves of memory flashed through my head and heart, making me realize it wasn't just memory—it was memory that ached. I was too scared to look back, but something felt odd yet familiar at the same time. Panic, amazement, and anxiety all hit at once—and then he absorbed them all by taking my hands in his.

"Yes" he said, his voice barely above a whisper.

"I" I managed to say the words, catching in my throat.

"Us" he completed, the simplicity of the word containing multitudes.

His arms encircled my tiny waist, holding me tightly. Then he pressed my hands against his so firmly that we might have swapped fingerprints. It felt warm and, for once in my life, extremely safe.

I closed my eyes and turned my face toward the bright blue sky. The hot sunlight bathed my skin while his hands, still holding mine tightly, made me feel more relaxed than I had in years.

We walked together silently, no words exchanged beyond those three: Yes, I, Us. What more needed to be said?

Later, as we sat in the garden of the old British colonial house with its sprawling acres planted with willows, mangoes, and tamarind trees, we began to speak of deeper things. The house had been my sanctuary, with poems of Wordsworth and Kipling etched into the ceilings. Monkeys, mongooses, and the occasional snake appeared—our own private nature reserve and mini zoo.

"For power, love, and my love—know to love first your source," I said, watching his expression carefully.

"That's deep thinking," he replied with a smile.

We had spent years learning from one another, from Greek letters to Brahmi script, from understanding family power dynamics to exploring philosophical concepts. Our conversations ranged from mathematics to mythology, from "pi to infinity" to Eternals, Nocturnals, X-Files, vampires, Pagan Roman witches of sorcery, magic wands and potions, fairies, and the most primordial energy as source energy.

And, of course, the concoctions.

I smiled with a grin at the memory of these wide-ranging.

"I love you. I am here for you. Even during hard times, I'll be here." Passed a handwritten tiny note onto my right hand.

For my beauty with golden proportions and golden ratio, and love,

A dusky Indian beauty where skin glows as yellow gold with a rich amber undertone, reminiscent of sun-kissed earth after a summer rain, as our first kiss. Your complexion glows with a natural warmth, ranging from goddess bronze to deep undertone of cinnamon, radiating vitality and depth. High cheekbones frame expressive eyes—often large and almond-shaped, with irises in captivating shades of deep brown and black like berry, which I kissed as you closed your eyes to sleep on my chest.

Your hair falls in luxurious waves or curls, typically raven-black with subtle undertones that catch the light as midnight moon or deep mahogany and reddish teak

Your features are harmonious – a defined nose with a gentle arch, full lips that curve naturally into an enigmatic smile, and a graceful jawline that completes your face's perfect symmetry. A natural elegance and timeless beauty to your gait, shoulders carried with quiet confidence.

Whether dressed in vibrant silks that complement your complexion or modern attire that embraces your heritage, you carry yourself with an effortless dignity that speaks to cultural roots and individual strength.

Your beauty transcends physical attributes, emanating from within—a magnetic presence, quiet wisdom reflected in eyes, and the resilient spirit of generations of women in our family before you.

My love,

I smiled, tilting my head slightly to the left and blew my favourite air kissed for soul kiss.

We decided to have coffee

"Generally, I take coffee with no sugar because of its bitterness," I said as he prepared our afternoon refreshments.

"You meant your kind of poison or the poison of the world?" he teased.

I took the demaru brown sugar and stirred it into my coffee, kissed the coffee mug, and smiled.

We moved to the veranda, settling on the carved wooden swing that faced the garden. The morning was still cool, though the promise of intense heat hung in the air. The scent of jasmine mingled with the rich aroma of our coffee.

I took a sip, feeling the warmth spread through me, and caught him watching me over the rim of his cup. His eyes held that familiar intensity—the look that had always made me feel both seen and desired.

"What?" I asked, knowing perfectly well what his gaze meant.

'And you spilled coffee on it,' I reminded him.

"The greatest accident of my life," he confessed. "It gave me an excuse to touch you."

I looked down at my watch, watching the surface ripple slightly with my breath. When I raised my eyes again, he had moved closer on the swing, his knee now touching mine.

I took another sip of coffee, deliberately letting a drop remain on my lower lip after slightly licking the one drop of spill outside the white coffee mug. His eyes followed the movement, darkening slightly.

"You have..." he began, motioning to my lip.

'I know,' I replied.

He set his cup on the small table beside us, then gently took mine and placed it beside his. With exquisite slowness, he leaned forward until his face was mere inches from mine. I could smell the coffee on his breath, mixed with his familiar scent—something uniquely his.

"May I?" he whispered, though we both knew permission had been granted long ago, in another lifetime.

I nodded slightly, and he closed the remaining distance. His lips met mine with gentle pressure, the taste of bitter coffee mingling between us. His hand came up to cup my face, his thumb tracing my collarbone with a reverence that made my heart beats faster and pulses racing as an athlete.

The kiss deepened as I parted my lips, inviting him closer. He tasted of coffee, desire, and memories—both sweet and bitter. My hands reached his chest, feeling his heartbeat accelerate beneath my palm. His other hand moved to my waist, pulling me closer on the swing.

We broke apart briefly for air, our foreheads touching, breath mingling in the small space between us.

"Coffee tastes better on you," he murmured, his voice lower now, roughened with want.

I reached for my cup, took another sip, and held the warm liquid in my mouth for a moment before kissing him again. The coffee passed between us, a shared intimacy that was both playful and profoundly erotic. His small gasp of surprise quickly transformed into a sound of pleasure as his hands tightened on my waist.

The swing creaked gently beneath us as the kiss intensified. His tongue traced the seam of my lips, seeking and finding entrance. The taste of coffee receded, replaced by his more intoxicating flavor—familiar yet somehow new after all our years apart.

My hands moved up to tangle in his hair. He pulled me closer until I was nearly in his lap, the thin fabric of my morning dress doing little to shield the heat between us. His hand traced a path from my waist to just below my breast, hovering there in question.

I answered by arching slightly into his touch, granting permission without words. Our mouths remained connected, and we had a conversation of lips and tongue, and we shared breath that said more than words ever could.

When his hand finally cupped my breast, the gentle pressure sent waves of sensation through me. I could feel my nipple hardening beneath the cotton, and he groaned softly into my mouth at the discovery.

"We should finish our coffee," I whispered against his lips, not meaning it at all.

"It's already finished," he replied, his eyes holding mine with an intensity that made my breath catch. "And we've waited fifteen years. I don't want to wait another moment."

I smiled, remembering how he had always been able to read my true meaning beneath the words. "Then don't," I said simply.

With elegance and refinement.

He returned my smile, understanding perfectly.

"We had messaged each other daily as we were growing up, our relationship evolving alongside technology. But it was the content rather than the medium that mattered—our last messages ramping up in intensity as we approached this reunion," as I said.

"Are you still wearing the ring from the family?" he asked suddenly.

"Yes, it is the circle of the eye of the tiger and sunlit as right and left, not right and wrong."

"No more wearing the show-stopper ring?" he inquired, referencing an ostentatious piece I'd once favored.

"Hands are not slim for the ring to slip," I smiled.

I watched him as he seemed to win hearts even among those who normally presented challenges. He had always had that gift—bringing people together across divides.

"Seeking a British break to have space in the most beautiful countryside to unwind?" he suggested.

"This is not sounding new," I responded.

"You meant '*nu*', '*nous*' in French?"

"*Sortie*," I said.

Just arrived,

"Gymshark or Sweaty Betty?" he asked, referencing athletic wear with a smile.

I simply smiled in response.

Our conversation shifted to more philosophical territory. We discussed how humans perceive love differently across different strata of society, depending on situations or state of mind. We talked about artificial intelligence, language models, and the ethics of teaching machines to understand human complexity, including moral consciousness, universal truth, and, most importantly, fundamental to human fabric, decency.

"Wish we were still in the society that sings and dances, feeling love as one love," he said wistfully.

"Tell me one letter—'la'—root of all love," I challenged.

"Not the thread—'coo'—root of all knots," he countered.

You meant the hug,

We smiled at our private language, which had developed over decades.

As the afternoon waned, our conversation turned to chess metaphors – always our favorite way to discuss relationships and power dynamics.

"Queen is more powerful even without the king; the King is powerful because the queen gives him moves," I explained.

"When a king loses or gets defeated, he might look like a pawn. The same king joins with another lost kingdom; they recover their dignity if not wealth."

He nodded, following my logic. "The same pawn who walked every step, evading every move or distracted by their queen or team, to reach the other end, they get two powerful queens."

"Powerful foot soldiers are hardworking soldiers with queens and chess members' protection," I continued.

"Queen skips many steps or fewer steps to strike that opponent, or for a stalemate or checkmate. Feels like a lioness missing a few steps for her hunt on the run. The cubs get licked and grabbed as her loyalists."

"When closer or feeling motherly or protecting the king, the king takes one step and makes that step to reach the number one position," he explained.

We connected our hearts and souls as one source. One source, not as fleeting as social media trends, but something eternal.

As evening approached, we wandered into the garden. A soft rain began to fall, but neither of us moved to go inside.

"Why are you kissing me?" I asked as his lips found mine beneath the raindrops.

"Because I like kissing you," he answered simply.

"For a kiss to wake up and a sweet kiss for good night," I murmured against his mouth.

"Just the day with you, dear," I teased.

"I love you."

"I love you."

"Take me to the sweetest cave," I whispered.

Later, as we watched the red moon of a partial solar eclipse, we admired the connection to our sun, a reflection of light, like the rising sun to the stars, and all random talks.

"I need you for today and every day, for eternity," he said, perhaps the most romantic line a woman can hear from her man.

We walked in comfortable silence for a while before he spoke again.

"Peaceful sleep is in the laps but on the hearts of the beloved."

I nodded, knowing this truth from experience.

And nothing was ever the same again.

We visited a nearby temple and shared a coconut dessert afterward. The temple visit was one of the finest moments in my life after living in such seclusion. I read the etched words: "Adi source love, Aran—value live, *aramuthe* (divine) forever."

"We have to be the source of love, and it has to rise from within," I said.

Later that evening, he asked me a question I hadn't expected.

"Why would you want to tie a knot and get married?" I asked him, curious about his reasoning after all these years.

"To kiss you every day," he replied with the silliness and sweetness that I had always loved.

"Would you like to travel around the world, and kiss on every beach in moonlight like high tides and low tides?" I said.

He smiled

"For a lifetime, as you set the standard for beauty both from within and outside."

I smiled, touched by his words.

"Being committed, safe and protective, rescuing each other in troubles, caring and supporting, having a drive in silent companionship as we age," he continued more seriously.

'People are a collective society, bringing collective wisdom,' I mused.

"Am I dating a politician?" I asked with a smile.

"In the first place, he has always been a politician," he replied.

"You mean my school captaincy and college elections," he said with a nostalgic smile.

"We missed those days."

'Love you,' he said simply.

'I love you,' my heart responded.

Soulfully, missing is kissing. There are many bodies, but you get soul-kissed or kiss the soul and heart to love as a soulmate.

"A stranger," I said, referring to how we began.

'A star is born as my star,' he replied.

"Welcome to the family," he said, opening his arms.

I smiled, finally feeling that I had found my place in the universe—not as two separate entities but as one unbreakable connection beyond time and space.

"First love, as genuine and everlasting, is a divine cosmic power," I thought but didn't say aloud.

'You are my trinity,' he said, as if reading my mind.

"Man of character and man of honor and man of wealth as collective wisdom, collective wisdom, and collective wealth," I said, watching his face carefully.

"The Politician is the finest man, Dear Love,"

They think it is other half or better half, not knowing the physical representation is for the mass to have godly understanding of goddess Shakti and God Shiva, and the spiritual representation is feminine and masculine energy not as equal half but as whole and half of self within as divine.

A resurrection as holiness,

Another, still my kind.

As First family, Family First,

As it all started, **Adi.**

# THE FLIGHT

**When Love Never Dies**

**Prologue**

"When love never dies - there are no goodbyes, no guilt! It is not the flames game of two names but an eternal connection between two souls beyond different worlds and times."

Romantic girls and ambitious boys rarely make suitable pairs in the practical world—this conventional wisdom had followed them throughout their relationship. They seemed destined for different paths, yet somehow their lives had become so deeply infused that bringing them back together would not be as 'TWO' but as 'ONE'.

## Chapter 1: Endings and Beginnings

### Morning, September, Dublin, Ireland

The most admired executive in the company, adored by the board of directors, left the conference room without uttering a single word. In the male-dominated world of tech finance, Sia had become a rare female star—"SHE" in the world of "HEs."

The decision had been made. After five years of building Infinity Frame Tech from a small startup into a £50 million enterprise, Sia had just witnessed the board vote for complete dissolution—not a restructuring or a merger, total liquidation. The company she had poured her life into would cease to exist by the end of the quarter.

She took the next flight to London Gatwick, her mind racing with possibilities and consequences. While waiting for her connection at the airport, she opened her purse and extracted a tiny blue velvet pouch. Inside lay a precious piece of jewelry worn only once in the last fifteen years—a Celtic knot pendant symbolizing enduring love with infinity. Rich or poor everyone had to tie that knot, one for relationship, one for family and one for our world. Is this thread under any sacred fire or with scared family with the knot of infinity gives a meaning knotted hearts.

Celtic knots, she remembered, were exchanged between two individuals to represent eternity, an endless path, never-ending faith, loyalty, trust, friendship, and love. This "love knot" meant more than an "I do." It transcended the traditional vows of "for better, for worse, to love and to cherish till death do us part." It symbolized crossing the passage even after death and making choices together, whether bound for hell or waiting for heaven.

Tears raced down her cheeks as grief poured through an uncontrollable stream. She hurriedly reached for tissues from her purse, trying to compose herself in the busy terminal.

She wore her favorite polka dot blue dress from the British brand Phase Eight, paired with comfortable black Clarks heels. As she walked through the concourse, she noticed several news reporters taking photographs and preparing to publish the morning headlines about the dissolution of Infinity Frame Tech. The impending liquidation of assets and settlement of outstanding debts raced through her mind, a constant undercurrent of stress beneath her carefully maintained exterior.

To avoid being pursued by persistent journalists, Sia quickly ducked into a restroom. She changed into the appearance of a typical college student – a purple Gap t-shirt and striped blue shorts. She meticulously removed her deep brown Chanel Rouge Allure lipstick, wiped away her light foundation, and removed all traces of her mascara.

As she stared at her transformed reflection, memories flooded back. The face looking back at her resembled the college girl she once was, not the polished tech executive she had become. She closed her eyes, allowing herself to be transported back to those days, when she first met Adi, when life seemed simpler and more complicated.

The weight of the Celtic knot in her hand brought her back to the present. She needed to see him now more than ever. After fifteen years, it was time to fulfill the promise of their eternal connection.

The hum of the private jet was a steady rhythm beneath her fingertips as she traced the rim of her untouched champagne glass. Outside, the world stretched endlessly, a sea of clouds dissolving into the night. The city she had built her life in was nothing more than a distant glow now, fading beneath the altitude.

She had been on countless flights, but tonight, something felt different.

Wealth had come fast. Faster than she had ever imagined. Deals, investments, and carefully played moves had placed her in rooms she once only read about. She had dined with billionaires, shaken hands with men who shaped the economy, and walked through the halls of power.

And yet, as she leaned back against the leather seat, there was an ache in her chest she couldn't ignore.

Her phone vibrated on the table beside her. A name flashed across the screen—**Abi**.

She inhaled sharply, her fingers hovering over the device. It had been years—years since she had last seen him, last heard his voice. Time had done nothing to dull the memory of their first meeting, nor had it erased the weight of what they once were. Twin flames, they had called it—a connection too deep to sever, too wild to tame.

But love, she had learned, was not enough.

She glanced at the jet's interior—polished mahogany, gold accents, a world far removed from where she started. She had everything she had once dreamed of. And yet, this message, this simple notification, unraveled something inside her.

She hesitated, then picked up the phone.

**Him:** *Are you still the girl I used to know?*

Her lips parted slightly. Was she?

She had spent years—someone untouchable, someone who had learned to wield power as effortlessly as a weapon. And yet, something in his words made her feel exposed, as if he could still see through the layers she had built.

The flight attendant approached, voice smooth and practiced. "Miss, would you like your drink refreshed?"

She barely heard her. Instead, she stared at the message, at the name on her screen, feeling the past collide with the present at 40,000 feet in the air.

With a deep breath, she pressed **reply**.

**Me:** Do you really want to find out?

As the jet soared higher, so did the ghosts of the life she had left behind.

This time, there would be no running.

# THE GIRL – FLASHBACK UNIVERSITY

The first time she realized she was different, she stood at the back of a crowded university lecture hall, watching her classmates settle into their familiar routines. Some were diligently taking notes, others were half-listening, their minds drifting toward weekend parties. But she-she was thinking of something else entirely.

Her name was **Sia**, and she had never been one to follow the ordinary path.

While others were concerned with grades and internships, she dreamed of something bigger: a life that extended far beyond this university's walls and the expectations her family placed upon her. But unlike those who only dreamed, she was determined to make it happen.

# A LIFE BETWEEN TWO WORLDS

Her parents wanted her to play it safe—study hard, get a stable job, and build a respectable life. But safe had never been enough for her. She longed for something grander, something that set her apart.

Yet, despite her hunger for success, there was another side to her. She was young, romantic, and deeply fascinated by love—not just any love, but the kind that was fated, magnetic, inescapable.

From the outside, she fit in—another university student juggling assignments, friendships, and fleeting moments of freedom. But beneath the surface, her mind was always in motion, mapping out a future that no one around her could understand.

She had always been observant, reading between the lines of people's conversations, noting who had real influence and who only pretended. The wealthy students who carried themselves with an effortless air of superiority fascinated her, not because she envied them, but because she studied them. She wanted to understand the unspoken rules of power, how success was more than just hard work—it was about positioning, timing, and knowing the right people.

Yet, she was not heartless. Beneath her calculated ambitions was a deep curiosity, a desire for something beyond material gain. Love was just as powerful to her when it is not feeling, an act of love and divine when you see each other, and cosmic when you are with one another. More than money, wealth, and any power, the world dictates. She believed that true love and true connection had the ability to transform, to elevate.

This belief was why she paid attention to the stories of twin flames and soul connections that defied logic. She had never experienced anything like it, but part of her—no matter how rational—hoped that one day, she would.

## A MEETING THAT CHANGED EVERYTHING

And then, she saw him. Not like I see, you see.

He wasn't like the others. There was something in how he carried himself—confident, but not arrogant; distant, yet entirely present. Their eyes met, and for a brief moment, it felt as if the world had tilted, as if something unseen had locked into place.

She wasn't one to believe in clichés, but she couldn't deny the pull between them. It wasn't just an attraction. It was something deeper, something unspoken.

And just like that, the life she had been so carefully building began to shift.

She didn't know it yet, but this was the beginning of everything.

'Good night,' he said.

'Good night,' I said.

For the rest of the evening, his presence lingered in her mind like an unsolved equation. She had met plenty of people—ambitious, charming, and wealthy—but there was something different about **him**. It wasn't just an attraction. It was a feeling she couldn't quite name, as if the universe had pressed pause the moment their eyes met.

She told herself she wasn't the type to get distracted. Her goals were clear: finish university, build connections, step into a world of her family where wealth and power dictated everything. Falling for someone—especially someone she barely knew—wasn't part of the plan.

But the feeling remained.

## A CHANCE ENCOUNTER

Two days later, she saw him again.

This time, it wasn't amidst a crowd but in the quiet classroom. She had been deep in a book of lectures about financial markets when she felt a shift in the air—an awareness that made her look up. He was sitting a few tables away, flipping through a thick hardcover, seemingly uninterested in anything around him.

Yet, as if he could sense her gaze, he glanced up. Their eyes met again.

It was ridiculous, she thought. A moment shouldn't feel like this – like an unspoken promise, a question waiting to be answered.

And then, just as she was about to look away, he did something unexpected.

He **smiled.**

It was a small thing, just a slight curve of his lips, but it sent a spark through her.

She hesitated, then forced herself to return the gesture before focusing back on her book. But the words on the page blurred. The numbers and market trends she had been analyzing moments ago no longer held the same weight.

**WHO WAS HE?**

She didn't know yet. But something told her that meeting him wasn't a coincidence.

## THE FIRST CONVERSATION

It wasn't until a week later that they spoke.

She was in a cafe just outside campus, waiting for her coffee, when she felt a presence beside her. Turning, she found him casually dressed but still carrying the quiet confidence that set him apart.

'?" he asked, nodding toward the book she had open on the counter.

She raised an eyebrow, surprised that he had noticed. "Something like that."

"Interesting choice," he mused, leaning against the counter. "Most people either love it or hate it."

She smirked. "And what do you think?"

He paused, studying her with an intensity that made her pulse quicken. "I think people who study finance don't just want money. They want control."

For a moment, she had no response because he was right.

She tilted her head. "And what do you study?"

His lips twitched, as if the question amused him. "Let's just say I prefer to learn outside the classroom."

A non-answer. Mysterious. Intriguing. Dangerous.

She knew she should walk away. But instead, she found herself saying, "Then maybe you can teach me something I won't find in a textbook."

# Chapter 2: The Encounter

Fate rarely announces itself. It moves in shadows, in coincidences too deliberate to be accidents yet too subtle to be recognized in the moment.

She didn't know it then, but something shifted in the universe the moment she met him.

It was a late autumn afternoon, and the sky was painted in soft golds and blues. She had been making her way across campus, her thoughts consumed by numbers, stock trends, and the growing certainty that it is much larger than life in the grand scheme.

And then—**him.**

She didn't notice him at first. He wasn't the type to demand attention, yet he carried a magnetic presence that was impossible to ignore for long. He leaned casually against a stone pillar near the entrance, flipping through a book he didn't seem to be reading. The afternoon sunlight caught the sharp lines of his face, illuminating eyes that held secrets she wanted to unravel.

Their gazes met.

For a second, time folded in on itself.

There was no grand revelation, no instant understanding of who or what he was to her. Only a feeling-a pull, deep and visceral, as if an invisible thread had looped around her ribs and tied itself to him.

She looked away first.

She wasn't a girl who believed in fate. But as she walked past, she could still feel his eyes on her, a weight that lingered long after she had turned the corner.

## AN INEVITABLE MEETING

Days passed, but that fleeting moment stayed with her. She told herself it was nothing – just a trick of the mind, an illusion created by her curiosity.

And yet, fate wasn't finished with them.

The next time she saw him, it wasn't in passing. It was a stormy evening, and she had sought refuge in a quiet cafe off campus, one of those dimly lit places where the coffee was strong and the world outside felt distant. She was flipping through her notes when a voice cut through the low hum of conversation.

"Finance again?"

She glanced up. **Him.**

He stood at the counter, one hand in his pocket, watching her with something between amusement and curiosity.

She arched an eyebrow. "Are you stalking me?"

He smirked. "If I were, do you think I'd make it this obvious?"

She rolled her eyes but couldn't help curling her lips at the edges.

He didn't wait for an invitation. Instead, he pulled out the chair across from her and sat down, setting his coffee on the table. Up close, he was even more infuriatingly compelling. There was a sharpness to him that hinted at danger—not in the reckless sense, but in the way he seemed to understand people too well, as if he could see the pieces of them they tried to hide.

He repeated it once, as if testing how it felt on his tongue. Then, he leaned back. "Interesting. You look like someone who's always five steps ahead."

"Is that your way of saying I seem calculating?"

"Not calculating," he mused. "Just... careful. Like you're always measuring people before you let them in."

She tilted her head, intrigued despite herself. "And what about you? What's your story for the day?"

He took a slow sip of his coffee before answering. "Abiends. Do you want the truth or the version that sounds better?"

The way he said it sent a shiver down her spine.

Something told her that no matter how much she thought she understood the world, he was going to prove her wrong.

She should have walked away.

Something about him set off quiet alarms in her mind—not warnings of danger, but of disruption. He was the kind of person who could rearrange the order she had carefully built for herself; the type who could make her forget why she had always preferred logic over emotion.

And yet, she stayed.

## AN UNSPOKEN UNDERSTANDING

Their conversation flowed in an effortless way, yet charged with something she couldn't quite name. He didn't speak like the others—didn't fill the silence with empty words or the usual questions about coursework and plans. Instead, he asked questions that felt personal, even when they weren't.

"What's the endgame for you?" he asked, stirring his coffee absentmindedly.

She frowned. "What do you mean?"

"I mean—what's all this for? The finance books, the careful planning, the ambition in your eyes. What do you really want?"

She hesitated. Most people never bothered to ask that. They assumed or they didn't care.

She could have given him the simple answer that made sense.

**SUCCESS. POWER. A LIFE WHERE NO ONE COULD TELL HER 'NO'.**

But that wasn't the full truth, was it?

"Freedom," she admitted finally. "The kind that only comes when you have enough money, enough influence, that the world stops feeling like a cage."

He studied her for a long moment before leaning back in his chair. "Interesting," she narrowed her eyes. "What?"

"You talk about freedom, but you don't seem like someone who actually wants to be alone."

The words hit deeper than she expected. She wasn't sure why, but how he looked at her—like he already knew things about her she hadn't even figured out herself—made her uneasy.

"You don't know me," she countered.

His lips curved, but it wasn't quite a smile. "Maybe not. But I know the way you're looking at me right now."

She blinked. "And how's that?"

"Like you don't know whether you want to run away from me or figure me out."

She let out a soft, disbelieving laugh. "You're really full of yourself, aren't you?"

"Not really," he took another sip of his coffee. "I just recognize the signs."

Something in his voice made her chest tighten.

Because the truth was, he wasn't wrong.

## THE FIRST IMPRINT

Their encounter ended before she was ready for it to.

After a few more exchanges—playful, some charged with meaning she couldn't quite decipher—he glanced at his watch and stood.

"I have somewhere to be," he said, his tone casual. "But I feel this isn't the last time we'll talk."

It wasn't a question.

She wanted to say something witty, something that would make it seem like she wasn't affected by this conversation, by **him.** But for the first time in a long time, she couldn't think of anything to say.

So, she just watched as he walked away, disappearing into the cool evening air.

And as she sat there, staring at the empty space he left behind, one thought ran through her mind.

## WHAT THE HELL JUST HAPPENED?

She had spent her whole life making calculated decisions. But something told her that whatever had just started between them, this wasn't going to be something she could control.

She told herself she wouldn't think about him.

It was a fleeting conversation, a moment in time that didn't deserve the space it was taking up in her mind. She had things to do—deadlines, exams, plans. And yet, no matter how hard she tried to push it away, she kept replaying their exchange.

The way he spoke to her was as if he had known her for years instead of minutes. He seemed unaffected by the world in the way only a certain kind of person could be—those who had already decided the rules didn't apply to them.

She didn't know if she liked that about him.

Or if she envied it.

## THE UNEXPECTED REUNION

Days passed. Then a week.

She convinced herself it had been nothing more than a strange moment – an interesting but ultimately meaningless interaction.

Then, one evening, she saw him again.

It wasn't at the cafe this time. It was at an exclusive networking event in the city, one she had managed to secure an invitation to after weeks of careful planning. It was the kind of place where future CEOs brushed shoulders with investors, where money and influence moved in invisible currents beneath the surface.

She had dressed the part – elegant but sharp, polished but not ostentatious. She wasn't here to be noticed; she was here to observe, to learn.

And yet, the moment she stepped into the dimly lit ballroom, her eyes landed on **him.**

He wasn't supposed to be here.

But there he was, standing near the bar, speaking to a man twice his age who seemed to be hanging onto every word. His posture was relaxed, his expression unreadable.

For the first time, she wondered—who **was** he, really?

She was still staring when his gaze flickered to hers.

For a moment, neither of them moved.

Then, just like before, he smiled.

A slow, knowing smile, like he had been expecting this. Like he had known she would be here before even she had.

Her breath caught.

It would have been easy to ignore him, to pretend she hadn't seen him. But something about that look—the challenge, the invitation—made her feet move before her brain could stop them.

She walked toward him, masking her curiosity with the kind of indifference she had perfected over the years.

He turned slightly as she approached, his attention shifting effortlessly from the man he had been speaking with to her.

"I was starting to think you were avoiding me," he said.

She arched an eyebrow. "I didn't realize I was supposed to be looking for you."

He chuckled, low and amused. "No, but you were thinking about me."

She tilted her head, giving him a smirk. "You sound awfully sure of yourself."

"I don't have to be sure. I can see it."

There it was again—that unnerving way he looked at her, as if he was reading between the lines of everything she wasn't saying.

She crossed her arms. "You never told me what you do."

He leaned against the bar, studying her for a moment before answering. "I invest."

"In what?"

A slow smile. "Opportunities."

It wasn't an answer. At least, not a real one.

She narrowed her eyes. "You're infuriating."

"I know."

She hated how much she wanted to keep talking to him.

## THE PUSH AND PULL

The evening passed in a blur of conversation and stolen glances. He never gave her full answers, always leaving just enough unsaid to keep her intrigued. And yet, the more she learned about him, the more she realized he was a contradiction—calm but intense, detached but observant.

By the end of the night, as she was preparing to leave, he caught her wrist lightly, stopping her.

"Tell me something," he said, his voice softer now, more serious.

She raised an eyebrow. "What?"

"Do you ever feel like you're meant for something... bigger?"

Her throat went dry.

She had spent her entire life chasing that feeling but never put it into words, not like that.

And yet, he had.

For the first time in a long time, she had no response.

He let go of her wrist, letting the moment between them. Then, with that same unreadable smile, he simply said:

"I'll see you around."

Then he was gone, disappearing into the crowd as if he had never been there at all.

She exhaled, steadying herself.

One thing was certain – this wasn't over.

Not even close.

She didn't see him for days after that night.

And yet, he was everywhere.

Not physically, but in the way her thoughts drifted toward him when she least expected it. Her mind replayed their conversation, searching for meaning in the things he hadn't said.

He had gotten under her skin.

And that—more than anything—annoyed her.

She had always been in control of herself, of her emotions, of the way she allowed people into her world. But he had slipped past her defenses without even trying. And, worse, he knew it.

Still, she wasn't about to chase after him. If fate had brought them together twice already, then surely it would happen again.

And it did.

## A NIGHT OF SECRETS

The party was small but exclusive—invite-only. It was the kind of gathering where people with influence at university discussed things that never made it into the news.

She wasn't sure how she had ended up here, but she wasn't the type to say no to an opportunity. She had long since learned that access was everything.

She was standing by the floor-to-ceiling windows, nursing a glass of wine, when she felt someone approach.

"You again," he said, his voice smooth and amused.

She turned, already knowing who it was before she saw him.

He was dressed differently tonight—still sharp, still effortless, but there was something more relaxed about him like he was completely at home in this world of quiet luxury.

She tilted her head. "Starting to think you're following me."

He smirked. "Or maybe we just move in the same circles."

"Doubtful," she murmured, taking a sip of her wine.

He studied her, his gaze sharp yet unreadable. "You're a strategist," he observed.

"Always thinking five moves ahead."

She didn't bother denying it.

"And yet," he continued, "something tells me you didn't plan for me."

That hit a little too close to the truth.

She exhaled through her nose, setting her glass on the nearby table. "You talk in riddles."

"You like it."

She scoffed. "Do I?"

His lips twitched. "You haven't walked away yet."

He had a point.

She should have.

She should have turned on her heel, left him standing there, and rejoined the party. But something about the way he looked at her made it impossible to move.

Like he was waiting for her to figure something out.

Like he already knew how this would end.

# THE CONFESSION

The night stretched on, and so did their conversation.

It wasn't like the small talk she had with others. It was layered, filled with silences that carried meaning, with words that danced on the edge of something deeper.

At one point, as the city glittered below them, she asked the question lingering in her mind since their first meeting.

"Why do I feel like I've met you before?"

He didn't answer right away. Instead, he studied her with an intensity that sent a shiver down her spine.

Then, quietly, he said, **"Because you have."**

Her breath caught.

For a moment, the world around them faded – the party, music, and glasses clinking. All that existed was him and the weight of those words.

She swallowed. "That's impossible."

"Is it?"

He wasn't smiling now. He wasn't teasing.

He was looking at her as if he knew something she didn't.

As if he had been waiting for this moment longer than she could possibly understand.

She should have laughed it off, rolled her eyes, and called him ridiculous.

But she didn't.

Because deep down, some part of her already knew.

This wasn't just a chance encounter.

This was something else entirely.

And nothing would ever be the same again.

# Chapter 3: Love & Soul

Falling for him wasn't a choice. It was an inevitability.

She had spent her entire life making careful, calculated decisions—always weighing the risks, always thinking five steps ahead. But with him, logic didn't apply. There was no strategy, no plan.

Just *feeling*.

And it was intoxicating.

## THE FIRST KISS

It happened late one evening.

They had spent hours walking through the city, their conversation drifting between sharp wit and quiet confessions. He challenged her in ways no one else ever had, making her rethink things she thought she understood.

She had never believed in fate. But standing there, beneath the glow of the streetlights, staring up at him, she felt something undeniable.

It was one of the places that recorded heavy rainfall. The rain starts and stops at its own will where the met department prediction, if any, will fail. It was one such season and will make even the most unromantic person fall in love. He and I were walking from outside the chemistry lab and warning ourselves mentally in each other's minds that we should call it a day and night. While walking from the chemistry lab toward my hostel room, torrential monsoon rain started. We were drenched in a matter of a few seconds.

It was so beautiful being trapped in the stillness of time and in a rainstorm. I was wondering if this was nature's ploy to unite. The yearning for each other was so wild and high. Suddenly, the whole campus lights shut down, and it became pitch dark. In my mind and heart, I knew this was the moment. Suddenly, like a storm, he held me so close, so hard that I felt crumbling inside. He was tall and sinewy, while I can't be termed slim but healthy, with certain right proportions, curvy hips, and average height for a girl. He held me so tightly that I felt him warm despite being drenched in the cold, torrential rain. And he placed his soft lips against mine. This part was my first dream kiss. My heart, instead of skipping beats, was racing. Slowly, we were kissing to the tunes of each other's racing heartbeats. Not only did I hear the heartbeats, but I also felt and shared them. The way we were kissing made it feel like neither of us was experienced, yet words like euphoria were realized during such moments. The universe watching would vouch that we were in a trance!

Slowly, the kissing was becoming stronger, and we were becoming irresistible to one another. Briefly, against my will, I pushed him away and ran a short distance to get out of the spell. He grabbed me again from my back and twisted me around like a can of Coke. With all his addiction, he kissed me strongly while grabbing & groping my soft left breast through the fabric of my dress. This is a time of addiction to love and lust, which we both couldn't resist. I knew this was going beyond a romantic kiss to lustful yearning. I could hear his breath as the desire further filled our hearts.

Though we were intoxicated by the love in the air as if we had known each other for many lifetimes, my mind was waking up and calling it perhaps a crush, lust, fatal attraction, and taking a promise from me never to meet again – Break away!

We were so drenched in rain and passion. He walked me through the rain, and I was returning.

'Good night,' he said.

'Good night,' I said.

Heat rushed through her, her heart pounding so hard she could feel it in her fingertips. She clutched his jacket, anchoring herself as the world blurred around them.

It wasn't just desire. It was recognition.

## THE HIGHS AND LOWS

Their connection burned fast.

Days turned into weeks, and she found herself caught in a whirlwind of stolen moments—late-night conversations that blurred into sunrise, whispered secrets that felt too raw to share with anyone else.

He saw through her in ways that terrified her. She had always been the one in control, the one who never let anyone close enough to hurt her. But with him, there was no hiding.

And for a while, she let herself believe that was enough.

But passion wasn't the same as stability. And love, no matter how intense, wasn't always enough to bridge the gaps between two people.

## THE CRACKS BEGIN TO SHOW

It started small.

A missed call. A late reply. A tension in the air that hadn't been there before.

She ignored it at first. She told herself she was imagining things.

But then there were the moments when he pulled away—not physically, but emotionally. When he looked at her as if he wanted to say something, but didn't.

She asked him once, late at night, as they lay side by side, bodies still tangled from the evening before.

"What are we doing?"

He exhaled, staring at the ceiling. "Living."

She frowned. "That's not an answer."

He turned to her then, his gaze unreadable. "Does it have to be?"

A part of her wanted to say yes, that love should come with certainty, that this feeling between them should have a name, a future, a plan.

But another part of her—the part that had always longed for something more—was afraid to push.

Because what if she did, and he wasn't ready to catch her?

## A LOVE THAT TRANSFORMED

He changed her.

Not in how people lost themselves in love, but in how love forced you to face the parts of yourself you'd rather ignore.

With him, she learned what it meant to be vulnerable.

To want something without knowing if she could have it.

To love without knowing if it would last.

And even though some of her feared how much power he had over her, she couldn't walk away.

Because twin flames weren't meant to burn alone.

And no matter how complicated, no matter how uncertain—

She wasn't ready to put out the fire.

Falling in love with him felt like standing at the edge of a cliff – terrifying and exhilarating all at once.

She had always prided herself on being rational, on never letting emotions dictate her choices. But with him, there was no logic. Just feeling.

It was all-consuming. Addictive. And no matter how much she tried to stay grounded, she was already in freefall.

## MOMENTS THAT DEFINED THEM

Their love was made up of stolen moments, of conversations that felt like secrets.

They would meet in quiet places—the rooftop of an old bookstore, the dimly lit cafe where they first spoke. Time never seemed to exist when they were together. Hours passed in heartbeats, nights spent tangled in sheets and whispered confessions.

She had never felt so seen.

He could read her like an open book, catching the thoughts she never spoke aloud. When she tried to hide, he called her out on it. When she built walls, he knocked them down.

And in return, she wanted to know everything about him – the parts he showed the world and the parts he kept hidden.

But she was starting to realize he wasn't ready to share some things.

## THE FIRST SIGNS OF DISTANCE

She noticed it one evening, long after the city had fallen asleep.

The warmth of their last kiss still lingered between them. She had curled up against him, her fingers tracing lazy patterns on his chest.

"Tell me something real," she murmured.

He exhaled softly, his hand brushing against her back. "Like what?"

"Something you've never told anyone."

For a long moment, he said nothing. She could feel the rise and fall of his breathing, slow and steady, but there was something else, too—something guarded.

Finally, he spoke.

"I don't believe in forever."

She blinked, pulling back slightly. "What do you mean?"

His gaze was unreadable. "Nothing lasts. Not love, not people. Everything fades eventually."

A lump formed in her throat. "You don't believe in love?"

He hesitated. "I believe in moments. I believe in this. But love is just a story we tell ourselves. Something that feels real until it isn't."

His words hit her harder than she expected.

Because she believed in love.

Not the fairy-tale kind, not the kind that promised perfection. But the kind that transformed, that built something lasting between two people.

And she had started to believe that maybe—just maybe—he was the person with whom she could have that.

But what if he never let himself believe it, too?

LOVING A STORM

The more she fell for him, the more she realized that loving him was like loving a storm.

Unpredictable. Beautiful. Dangerous.

Some days, he was all in—his touch urgent, his words pulling her deeper into his orbit. Other days, he was distant, lost in thoughts he refused to share.

She told herself it didn't matter. That what they had was enough.

Was she loving someone who would never let himself be caught?

And if so... how long could she keep pretending that wouldn't break her?

She tried not to let his words haunt her.

"I don't believe in forever."

They were just words. And words, she told herself, didn't always mean what they seemed.

But something about the way he had said them—his voice quiet, almost resigned—settled deep in her chest like an ache she couldn't shake.

She wanted to believe that if she loved him enough, if she showed him that love wasn't just a fleeting illusion, he would change. That he would wake up one day and realize that not everything faded. That some things—some people—were worth holding onto.

But love, no matter how strong, could not rewrite someone's past.

And his past, she was beginning to realize, was full of ghosts.

## LOVE THAT BURNS

They didn't talk about that night.

Instead, they did what they always did.

They felt.

Their love was fire–wild, uncontainable. It didn't grow gently; it consumed.

They met in stolen hours, their bodies tangled, their lips desperate, as if trying to say things that words couldn't.

She had never wanted anyone the way she wanted him.

It wasn't just the physical pull, though that was undeniable. It was the way he made her feel like the rest of the world didn't exist when they were together.

He would press his forehead against hers after kissing her breathless, his fingers running through her hair as if he were memorizing her. He would whisper things in the dark that made her shiver, things that made her believe that maybe, just maybe, he needed her just as much as she needed him.

For a week afterward, Sia replayed that evening in her mind countless times. They didn't meet again outside of class, though their eyes frequently found each other across the lecture hall. An unspoken understanding passed between them with these glances—an acknowledgment of what had happened and mutual recognition of their obstacles.

Their different backgrounds loomed large: she from a traditional family with clear political expectations about her future, he from a conservative family. Their connection, however genuine, existed in opposition to family traditions, community expectations, and a lifetime of ingrained beliefs.

But then, unexpectedly, everything changed.

## Chapter 3: Breaking and Mending

"Heartbreaking are the breakups that always end up with a passionate kiss, and blissful are the patch-ups that start with a passionate kiss."

Though it was a breakup in my mind, her heart convinced her it could be love forever with the moments they'd shared.

"Adi is waiting for you outside!" Meera's voice echoed through the hallway the next evening, a hint of playful teasing in her tone.

Sia felt her heart skip. After a week of exchanged glances and deliberate avoidance, she hadn't expected this. She checked her reflection quickly, smoothed her dress, and walked outside with practiced nonchalance that belied her racing pulse.

Adi stood by the entrance, his black shirt in stark contrast to the pale hostel walls. Without speaking, he began walking, finding his way to the curb outside the library where students often gathered between classes. The evening air was heavy with unspoken words.

"I wanted to talk," he finally said, his voice steady, but his eyes fixed on the ground before them. "About us."

I nodded, steeling myself. The strange premonition of what was coming didn't make it any easier to hear.

"I think..." he hesitated, choosing his words carefully. "I think we should keep this relationship simple. Let's be friends."

Though she summoned all her strength for this conversation, the words still cut deeper than anticipated. The proposal of friendship after the intimacy they'd shared felt impossibly inadequate, like offering a thimble to collect an ocean.

"When it has come down to this," she said, her voice remarkably steady despite the tremor in her chest, "I have no choice but to reject your proposal of being friends. How can we be friends after all that we shared? It rips my heart to say maybe we should not be meeting or talking again. I can't be just friends after what was between us."

They walked away from each other that evening, their paths diverging like rivers that briefly converged only to split again, each carrying traces of the other's current.

The weeks that followed were an exercise in exquisite torture. Every class they shared became a battlefield of restraint where silent battles raged beneath the veneer of academic focus. They couldn't stop exchanging glances across the lecture hall, as if every cell in their bodies yearned for connection. She would feel his eyes on her and look up to find him watching, sometimes with his head resting on his desk to maintain his uninterrupted gaze, his dark eyes conveying what words had failed to express.

During one particularly tedious lecture on fluid dynamics, their eyes locked for so long that Sia felt physically pulled toward him. Her brain waged war with her heart, her body, her soul—every part of her screaming to simply rise from her seat, cross the classroom, and surrender to the magnetic attraction between them. In that second, all rational thought dissolved, and all she wanted was to walk straight to him and kiss him, regardless of consequences.

They were only broken from this spell when Professor Murthy called on Adi to answer a question, drawing the curious attention of their classmates to his momentary confusion. A few students glanced between them, noticing the intensity of their exchange, which only heightened Sia's embarrassment.

Later, she forced herself to concentrate during classes, knowing these hours were her only chance to absorb information for upcoming exams. Her academic future couldn't afford the luxury of romantic distraction, yet concentration remained elusive whenever Adi was nearby. She developed a system of taking meticulous notes, hoping the mechanical action of writing would anchor her thoughts away from him and toward her education.

"You need to focus," her roommate Meera advised one evening, watching Sia struggle through her thermodynamics assignment. "Your scholarship depends on maintaining your GPA." And you have to have this scholarship for all political reasons, given the family

"I know," Sia sighed, rubbing her temples. "It's just—"

"Just nothing," Meera interrupted firmly. "Whatever is between you two can wait. Your future can't."

Sia nodded, knowing her friend was right. Yet even as she redoubled her efforts at studying, the undercurrent of awareness remained – a constant, humming tension whenever they occupied the same space.

Then, one morning during breakfast, everything shifted again. Their friends had congregated at the college canteen, and somehow Sia found herself sharing a plate of crepes with Adi. Their fingers occasionally brushed as they both reached for the same piece, each touch sending quiet electricity through her.

The next day in class, they exchanged stares and smiles across the lecture hall, their unspoken communication more eloquent than any words. When class finished at noon, Adi approached her desk.

"Would you join me for a walk?" he asked, his voice casual, but his eyes intense.

They strolled out together and decided to visit their private beach along the national highway, taking their favorite path. The summer day blazed hot around them, the air thick with humidity and unspoken intentions. Though no music played, Sia felt melodies in her head, a soundtrack to their complicated dance.

They found their favorite tree among the grove of pines lining the sandy shore. Sia sat beside him, his arms wrapping around her, pulling her close to his chest. The steady rhythm of his heartbeat against her back provided comfort she hadn't realized she'd been missing.

"Have you ever wondered about moments like this?" she asked, her voice barely audible above the whisper of waves.

"Yes," he replied simply.

Without further words, he began kissing her deeply as she rested her head on his lap. Time suspended itself around them, the world narrowing to the points where their bodies connected. When they finally pulled apart, both slightly breathless, Sia looked toward the horizon.

"I've never seen a sunset on a beach," she confessed, suddenly aware of all the experiences they had yet to share.

"Do you want to watch the sunset with me?" Adi asked, his voice holding a note of tenderness she rarely heard.

"Yes," she said, the single word carrying the weight of promises neither dared to make.

## Chapter 4: First Light

It was 6:00 pm when Sia checked her watch, the small gold timepiece her grandmother had given her before she left for university. The sun hung low over the horizon, casting golden light across the white sand that stretched for miles along the coastline. Adi stood beside her, his hand reaching for hers with a hesitance that betrayed his confidence in every other aspect of life.

"We should head back soon," he said, though his feet remained planted in the sand next to hers. "The pathway gets dark quickly after sunset."

Sia nodded but made no move to leave. This moment—the glow of orange light reflecting off the gentle waves, the warmth of his hand in hers—felt too precious to surrender to time. They met three weeks earlier in Professor Sharma's Comparative Literature seminar, where their passionate debate about modernist poetry had extended beyond class hours.

"Just a few more minutes," she whispered, squeezing his hand.

The magnificent sun, a perfect orange sphere, descended slowly into the sea, as if reluctant to end its day together. As the last sliver of light disappeared along the horizon, a subtle shift occurred between them—something unspoken yet undeniable.

They clasped hands and began the journey back along the narrow path where both sides were covered by tall and wild pine trees. The darkness settled around them quickly, the path ahead barely visible. Though it appeared menacing in the near pitch darkness, Sia found comfort in Adi's presence beside her. He seemed to sense her thoughts, pulling her closer to his side.

"You're quite safe with me," he murmured, his voice carrying a new depth in the darkness.

Sia had never considered herself someone who needed protection. Yet something about surrendering to this moment, to him, felt liberating rather than constraining.

They continued in compatible silence until they reached a bend in the path where the trees created a perfect canopy above them. The moonlight filtered through in scattered patterns across the ground. Adi stopped suddenly, turning to face her. His expression held both certainty and a question as he studied her face.

"I've wanted to do this since that first argument about C.S. Lewis," he said with a small smile.

Before she could respond, he pulled her softly toward him and pressed his lips to hers. Sia's eyes closed instinctively, her mouth remaining closed at first as her mind processed the sensation. His kiss was both gentle and insistent, asking rather than demanding. Time seemed to suspend itself around them, and she wished desperately for these seconds to last forever.

They continued along the path, stopping frequently to reconnect through kisses that grew increasingly passionate. Halfway to the highway, they reached a small bridge spanning a narrow stream.

When he pressed his lips harder, my lips parted. The fire in us was so ignited that he pulled me as if he was taking the whole of me inside his life. There was this tiny bridge halfway before the narrow pathway ends and connects to the national highway. Without stopping to kiss each other, he sat down on the bridge while I wrapped my legs around him. The need for wanting each other was rising just like high tides on a full moon night. Against the backdrop of moonlight, the raging kiss due to wild attraction in the most romantic place on earth was unstoppable. I felt his teeth bite my tongue softly. He kissed my neck, and my heart was all aflutter while my arms were getting numb holding him tight. He leaned on me, kissing my neck, while I leaned on him as if we were dancing to the sea waves.

In our minds, we were our naked selves while he and I were fully dressed. The nakedness is the emotional attachment, a feeling deeper where all flaws, differences, likes, and dislikes of the real world hold no meaning. For me, when love is there, the willingness to be one and like each other comes naturally, and life is about learning. The more the differences, the more the learning and adventure!

His kisses traveled lower, across her throat and collarbone, while his hands gently caressed her through her cotton blouse. She could feel his restraint, his respect for boundaries even in this moment of abandon. When his lips brushed against her chest and his arms encircled her, she twisted slightly, digging her fingers into his thick hair and pressing him closer. Even in the near darkness, she could see his eyes were closed, lost in the moment just as she was.

The pleasure built within her in unexpected waves, causing her to arch backward slightly. He savored each response as if memorizing her reactions for posterity.

"Adi," she moaned softly, unable to form his full name.

'Sia,' he responded, pulling her even closer.

For me, this transcended physical desire; it was about a deeper connection where worldly differences held no significance. Her philosophy had always been that other aspects fall naturally into place when love exists. Life was about learning, and differences only added to the adventure.

"I smiled," she whispered, once they had stilled somewhat.

"I smiled sinfully," he replied, the moonlight catching the gleam in his eyes.

Sia found herself speechless, wondering if it was possible to be consumed entirely by love. Half-expecting declarations or promises, she waited, but they didn't come.

Strangely, words seemed unnecessary in the face of what they had just shared.

Eventually, they continued their walk back toward the university. Outside, they paused one final time.

"Good night," he said simply.

"Good night," she replied, equally sparing with words.

I replayed that evening in her mind for a week afterward, countless times. They didn't meet again outside of class, though their eyes frequently found each other across the lecture hall. An unspoken understanding passed between them with these glances—acknowledgment of what had happened and mutual recognition of their obstacles.

Though I ended up going to bed fondly, remembering every tiny motion and moment, I was equally convinced that it would never work, given our backgrounds.

## THE SECRETS BETWEEN THEM

It started with small things.

A hesitation before answering a question. A flicker of something unreadable in his eyes when she mentioned the future. The way he would disappear for hours without explanation.

She didn't want to be the kind of girl who asked too many questions.

So, she let it go.

Until she couldn't.

# A MOMENT THAT CHANGED EVERYTHING

It was supposed to be a normal evening.

They had planned to meet at his place after one of her networking events—just another night of whispered conversations.

But when she arrived, he wasn't there.

At first, she didn't think much of it. He had always been unpredictable, his life full of things he never fully explained.

## Chapter 4: The Pendulum

"Expression of love is supporting and being there for each other, both during good times and bad times."

By now, Sia was slowly learning that love without lust, or lust without love, never truly worked—both elements needed to exist in harmony for something lasting to grow.

She tried to form the words to tell him, but he began talking about films he'd watched, particularly mentioning one he'd walked out of halfway through.

"I just left halfway through the movie," he said casually.

"Really?" she replied silently, "Perhaps we could continue the rest in real life."

The wind whipped her hair across her face, and she caught him watching her with an intensity that felt possessive, consuming. She lost herself in his gaze, struggling to focus on his words as he quickly shifted topics to discuss the political maneuvering happening in the election campaigns.

Coming from a limited social background, Sia struggled to understand the complex dynamics of politics, much less offer strategic advice. Instead, she listened attentively, communicating her support in the clearest way she knew.

"I am there for you, whatever times – good, bad, or ugly," she told him simply.

Their conversation touched on many dimensions of campus life, but Sia found joy simply in being together again. As the sun began setting on the horizon, they walked and talked, moving between various planted areas across the college grounds. Eventually, evening descended, and they found themselves at their favorite spot outside the chemistry lab—a location that seemed to amplify the burning desires between them.

The campus was brightly lit, and Sia could see him smiling with his lips pressed together in that particular way she'd come to recognize as a prelude to a kiss. Her heart pounded not with anxiety but anticipation as he leaned forward, covering her face with kisses before finding her lips, which parted readily for him. She responded with equal passion until the sound of approaching footsteps forced them apart.

The longing in his eyes was unmistakable as they hastily retreated, running a distance to avoid discovery. They made their way along the narrow path to the open-air auditorium. Their resistance to one another had completely crumbled. Adi pressed her against the wall in the backstage area, their kisses deepening with newfound urgency. When he lowered her to the floor, they continued their embrace, rolling without breaking contact. He positioned himself above her, hands planted on either side, simultaneously kissing and enclosing her in a protective cage of his arms.

Sia knew they were approaching a point of no return. If they didn't stop now, the consequences could be far-reaching.

"Sia," he whispered her name so tenderly she felt his breath against her face.

'Adi,' she replied, her voice quivering with emotion.

They eventually pulled themselves together, and he walked her back.

"Good night," she said with a smile.

'Sweet dreams,' he replied, his pressed lips curving into an expression that seemed both hopeful and expectant.

What was that expression, she wondered as she closed her door. Hopeful? Expectant? Whatever it was, it made her feel both treasured and uncertain.

## Chapter 5: Family Fractures

After class the next day, she informed Adi of her urgent travel home. He was wearing her favorite navy shirt, though it resembled a lab coat in its clinical formality. His mind seemed elsewhere, still dwelling on his election disappointment.

Sia listened attentively, but her thoughts drifted to her family's situation and her increasingly uncertain relationship with Adi. She couldn't determine whether what they shared was love, lust, or mere infatuation from childhood to their teenage days. The emotional turmoil was overwhelming.

Perhaps she needed solitude – the state where she had always found strength to rebuild herself.

When Sia returned from her family visit, a strange avoidance pattern emerged between them. Neither seemed eager to talk, though they exchanged occasional glances during classes.

One morning after a particularly tedious day, Adi approached her. "Would you like to join me for coffee and a snack?" he asked, his tone casual as if their passionate encounters had never happened.

They walked together to the main building cafeteSia, which overlooked the beach. The autumn season had arrived, bringing misty air and strong winds that tossed Sia's hair wildly. She caught Adi watching the spectacle with amusement.

"Moon Shot," he said with a hint of mischief.

Sia's limited understanding didn't include this sensitive term. When she asked for clarification, his explanation made her blush furiously. She laughed to mask her embarrassment – a defense mechanism she'd perfected over years of hiding insecurities.

The realization that she loved him had transformed her thoughts – his presence in her consciousness was constant, like breathing. She began discussing him and their relationship with her roommate, Meera, seeking validation for feelings she couldn't fully articulate.

Word traveled quickly.

"From my point of view, when we are in love, it is only natural to talk about and proudly declare our partners to friends and family," she tried to explain.

The transition from feeling like family to feeling like strangers in a matter of weeks was torturous. Sia began to doubt her earlier certainty, wondering if what they shared was love at all, or merely some vague, clandestine affair.

Days passed with their usual wordless exchanges of glances.

A new routine emerged: evening shower, dinner, and then a meeting for what Sia privately termed their "dose of addiction." During these encounters, Adi seemed completely lost in her, and the moment they came together, they would kiss with an almost violent urgency, unaware they were causing each other as much pain as pleasure.

Sia wanted to resist him but found herself unable to.

"Are we having an emotional companionship or a secret affair?" she wrote. "Sometimes you treat me like a princess on a pedestal, while other times I feel lowered and controlled by you. It's always your decision when we meet. I think this relationship should end because I don't have the mental strength to continue."

They walked away from each other once more.

## Chapter 6: Parallel Journeys

"Journeys that should never end"

It was the start of the summer holidays. By coincidence, Sia and Adi were traveling on the same day and on the same train.

Sia felt tongue-tied, having barely spoken to him since their last parting. But after they met on the train, within seconds they embraced and kissed as if no time had passed, as she rested her head on his shoulder. Were they so intoxicated with one another? Despite their exhaustion, they managed to stay awake the entire night, though they exchanged a few meaningful words. They kissed and nearly made love, restraining themselves only because of their surroundings.

The next morning, Sia left her seat as the train approached her station.

He responded with only a vague smile, and they walked away in opposite directions.

In that moment, Sia realized the depth of her feelings: "I was always attracted to him, but now I'm truly in love with him—it's beyond mere infatuation."

During the two-month summer break, she read every romance novel she could borrow from the local library, learning about relationships and intimacy primarily through the pages of Mills & Boon books.

Each day brought emotional turmoil as she expected some communication from him – a letter or a phone call. But there was no sign of any contact. Frustrated and hurt, she wrote him a long, emotional letter, expressing how he had made her feel diminished by sharing intimate moments and then never bothering to check on her during the holidays. Her emotional pendulum swung wildly as she questioned whether he truly liked her, loved her, or missed her at all.

When they returned to university, Adi called Sia after reading her letters. They planned to meet that evening.

"I need to talk to someone who can not only hear me but also listen deeply," she said when they met, her voice tense with suppressed emotion.

"Do you understand? Do you even understand what I feel?" she asked, her tone revealing her annoyance.

"I'm glad we're fighting," he said unexpectedly.

The response caught her off guard. "I'm glad you're putting up with the fight," she replied.

All Sia wanted was a more meaningful relationship with some sort of commitment. But no expression of love in words, let alone commitment, was forthcoming. Was he worried my father might not accept, or did he need approval from the godfather? They abandoned the difficult conversation and, as had become their pattern, kissed each other passionately.

## Chapter 7: The Breaking Point

"Family breaks, happiness breaks too."

Sia received separate calls from her parents every evening, learning how her family—her entire world—was falling apart. She took it all personally, skipping meals and neglecting self-care. Gradually, she developed health issues—migraines and neurological conditions that led to constant headaches and nausea, which caused her to skip even more meals.

One evening, as she was heading out to seek medical help for an unbearable migraine, she coincidentally ran into Adi, who took her to the hospital.

"Is there anything I should know? Anything you want to tell me?" he asked as they waited.

"Nothing," she said, unwilling to burden him with her family troubles.

He kissed her forehead and helped her dress after she received intravenous treatment. She wanted him to stay with her.

Her father flew in the next morning, visibly shaken by the situation at home and work. Seeing him in such distress.

Upon returning from the hospital, one of Sia's favorite seniors warned her against continuing her relationship with Adi, cautioning that it would only lead to more stress since it clearly wasn't developing in any meaningful direction.

Sia returned home and was prescribed antidepressants along with her migraine medication. She limited her interactions with Adi as much as possible.

Despite the emotional turbulence of love, breakups, and exam nights, Sia managed to complete university without academic failures, mostly maintaining decent grades—a far cry from her high school days when her near-perfect scores in science and mathematics came from pure studiousness and discipline.

During the college festival season, while Adi participated in theatrical productions, Sia focused on getting adequate rest and sleep.

After one performance, during which Adi experienced a particularly embarrassing situation, Sia waited in the empty auditorium after everyone had left, wanting to offer comfort and express her care for him.

They walked together, talking briefly. She had decided to make him feel like a man who had his girl beside him through difficult moments. With only mild passion, they kissed in a comforting manner. One thing led to another, and they shared their first truly intimate moment. Strangely, it felt uncomfortable for both, prompting them to separate. Sia left feeling unsettled, and they avoided each other for weeks afterward.

During the final year laboratory examinations, both Adi and Sia had difficult days.

Sia discussed these troubles with her closest friends at the girls' hostel, but felt judged by their remarks.

That evening, after Adi called, they met to talk. Neither was in the mood to listen to the other's problems, so they decided to break up and stop communication entirely. Sia returned to her hostel alone.

After taking her antidepressant and migraine medication, she fell asleep. Later that night, she learned Adi had been in an accident but was told not to visit him during late hours.

When she inquired about the accident, Adi displayed unpleasantness toward her, making her wonder if their breakup had somehow contributed to his accident. Nevertheless, she remained calm and stayed to comfort him, watching an old movie together. After a few hours of conversation, they kissed as usual before she left.

She visited again the following evening, sitting beside him on the hospital bed. He grabbed her and kissed her deeply, causing his IV to dislodge and blood to flow into his drip. Shocked, Sia called for a nurse. She realized she should leave – they simply couldn't keep their hands off each other, regardless of time, place, or circumstance.

## Chapter 8: Final Goodbyes

"It is not saying anything but still knowing all endings are signs for new beginnings."

As graduation approached, many students prepared for standardized tests like the GRE and GMAT. Sia took a more relaxed approach, focusing on completing her degree before deciding on her next steps. Despite judgmental views from others, she knew this was the right choice for her well-being.

During a trip to Goa with her female friends, Sia purchased a bright pink sarong skirt and a blue flowery top for herself. She considered buying something for Adi, but didn't know his shirt size. Instead, she decided to present herself as his gift, wearing her new outfit.

After several sleepless nights cramming for exams with her study partner, Sia and Adi began having long, intimate phone conversations from midnight until morning.

During one such late-night chat, they planned to meet at 5:00 am to watch the sunrise, just before their final examinations.

They walked together along the beach, finding their favorite spot among the pine groves. Sia, who couldn't swim, was afraid to enter the ocean but loved nature enough to wade in ankle-deep while Adi watched from the sandy shore.

'You look great no matter what you're wearing,' he said admiringly.

She asked him to lift and carry her, prompting him to "figure out something special." Though they kissed each other passionately, Adi seemed restrained despite the privacy of the early morning beach. Sia sensed something holding him back, a decision not to fully commit to her.

They began discussing their relationship and its future. This time, they mutually agreed not to continue beyond graduation. Sia had anticipated this conclusion and accepted it, though secretly she had hoped he might change his mind and stay connected. With her pride at stake, she didn't call him either. They sorrowfully agreed this was truly "the end."

After graduation, Sia moved to Chennai with her parents. Despite living with her family, she felt profoundly alone without Adi in her life. Two months passed without contact between them.

She considered investing in a firm across countries, funded partly by her father and partly through investors, but didn't want to leave the country or distance herself from him. She wanted to confess her feelings and become a part of his life.

They met at his place and talked briefly about her family situation and future plans on his terrace. A power outage interrupted their conversation, so they went out for dinner before he dropped her off at her place.

Weeks later, he called and visited her apartment. Their conversation gave way to passion as he gently kissed her lips while urgently removing her clothes, his actions mirrored by hers.

With her eyes closed, she surrendered to his touch on her skin, which sent electric sensations through her body. They were ready to make love, and she noticed a small smile cross his lips as he reached for protection. But their desire overtook their patience. His strong hands gripped her while his mouth covered hers hungrily, pushing her onto the bed. Fully naked, they joined together until he suddenly withdrew, not completing their union. The desperate sounds, the scent of him surrounding her—it all felt like an exquisite pleasure tinged with ache.

After dressing, they began discussing their future, but Sia was shocked to learn he was leaving town. Furious and defensive, she mentioned her new local friends with exaggerated enthusiasm. Realizing he wasn't prepared to commit, she echoed what she thought he wanted to hear, protecting her pride.

"I'm not thinking of you as my husband now," she said coolly.

"That's fine," he replied.

She had forgotten her scarf, which he pointedly mentioned, but she cared little for such details now. She waved goodbye with an aching heart.

She bitterly reflected that she deserved flowers at her doorstep, notes on her dashboard, calls, emails, love notes—all the romantic gestures that never materialized. The connection between them was flickering, the thought of love fading.

This was when she had to decide whether they were "meant to be" or "not meant to be."

# Chapter 4: Heartbreak

Love was supposed to be enough.

That was what she had believed—what she had wanted to believe. That if two people felt something undeniable, something bigger than themselves, it would be enough to hold them together.

But she had been wrong.

Because sometimes, love wasn't about how deeply you felt for someone.

Sometimes, it was about timing. About choices. About all the things that love alone couldn't fix.

And now, standing alone in the middle of a crowded world, she was finally beginning to understand that.

## THE AFTERMATH OF GOODBYE

She didn't see him after that night.

She thought she would. She had expected him to call, explain, show up, and tell her that what they had still mattered.

But days passed. Then weeks.

And the silence became its own answer.

She told herself she was fine, that she had survived worse, and that this was just another lesson, another scar to wear beneath the surface.

But the truth was, she had never felt emptier.

Because he hadn't just left—**he had taken a part of her with him.**

## DROWNING IN THE PAST

She threw herself into work, into distractions, into anything that kept her from thinking about him.

But grief wasn't something you could outrun.

It found her in the smallest moments—the familiar scent of his cologne lingering on a sweater she had forgotten to return. The songs that played in cafes reminded her of nights spent tangled in sheets and whispered secrets.

She hated that he still existed in the details of her life.

Hated that no matter how far she tried to run from him, his absence was still a presence.

And worst of all, she hated that she wasn't sure she *wanted* to forget him.

## THE SEARCH FOR ANSWERS

One night, after too many sleepless hours, she found herself doing something she swore she wouldn't.

She searched for him.

Not just in old messages or photos, but in the places where power moved.

Because if he didn't give her answers, she would find them herself.

And what she found made her blood run cold.

He wasn't just wealthy.

He wasn't just connected.

He was tied to something far bigger—something with shadows that stretched into the kind of world she had only ever heard whispers about.

A world where love wasn't enough.

A world where feelings were dangerous.

And suddenly, she understood.

He hadn't left her because he didn't care.

He had left her because **loving him meant walking into something she might never escape.**

And now, she had a choice.

Let him remain a ghost in her past.

Or find out what he had been protecting her from all along.

**And for better or worse, she had never been the kind of woman who walked away without answers.**

# Chapter 5: First Steps

Heartbreak had changed her.

It had stripped away the last remnants of the girl who believed in love above all else. What remained was sharper, more focused. She had spent too long waiting for answers, for closure that never came.

Now, she wasn't looking for love.

She was looking for power for her family.

Because if she had learned anything from losing him, it was this: **control meant never being left behind again.**

TO BUILD THE BRIDGE, TO BRIDGE THE GAP, BEFORE BUILDING THE BRIDGE

## A DOOR INTO A NEW WORLD

It started with an invitation.

A name she didn't recognize. A location she had only heard whispered about.

It arrived in the form of an elegant black envelope, slipped into her hands by a woman whose presence felt just as deliberate as the message itself.

*"You've been noticed,"* the woman had said, her voice smooth. *"You should come."* She almost didn't. Almost convinced herself that this wasn't her world.

But then, she thought about him. About the questions he had left behind. About the power he had wielded so effortlessly.

And she realized—maybe it had been her world all along. She had just been waiting for the right moment to step into it.

So, she went.

## THE FIRST TASTE OF INFLUENCE

The event was unlike anything she had ever seen.

It wasn't just a party—it was an **ecosystem** of the world's most powerful people. Bankers, CEOs, tech moguls, and investors who moved money in ways that reshaped industries.

Everything was unspoken, yet understood.

Deals were made over glasses of champagne. Fortunes were exchanged with a handshake. Influence was the real currency, and only those who knew how to wield it were allowed inside.

She watched. She listened. She learned.

And as the night went on, she realized something.

She wasn't just there to observe.

She was there because someone had decided she belonged.

## A MYSTERIOUS OFFER

Near midnight, as the city lights stretched below them, she found herself standing on a terrace, staring out at a skyline that no longer felt unreachable. "You fit in here."

She turned.

A man stood beside her, older and refined—one of those people whose presence carried weight without needing to be announced.

"I'm just here to watch," she said smoothly. He smiled, amused. "No one is ever *just* watching."

She didn't respond.

After a moment, he reached into his jacket and handed her a card.

"Come and see me when you're ready," he said.

She glanced at the card. No name, just an address.

When she looked up, he was already walking away.

And in that moment, she knew—

This was it.

The first step toward something bigger. Toward a world where power wasn't just something you admired from a distance.

It was something you took.

**And she was ready.**

She held the card between her fingers, its weight heavier than it should have been. No name, just an address. An invitation—not just to a meeting, but to something far bigger.

She had a choice.

She could walk away and return to the life she had carefully built, or she could step forward, take the risk, and see just how far she could go.

There was no hesitation.

The next evening, she arrived at the address.

It wasn't an office or a club or anything she had expected. It was a penthouse—a fortress of glass and steel, towering above the city. She was led inside by a woman who spoke only in gestures, guiding her through halls lined with art that likely cost more than entire buildings.

And then she saw him.

The man from the party.

Sitting at a marble table, sipping something dark from a crystal glass, watching her as if she were the most interesting puzzle he had ever encountered.

"You came," he said simply.

She nodded. "I don't waste opportunities."

A slow smile. "Good. Then let's begin."

# A LESSON IN POWER

The conversation wasn't casual.

He spoke in riddles, testing her, seeing how she thought and reacted. Every question felt like a challenge, and she answered each one with sharp, calculated answers.

"Power isn't about money," he said at one point. "It's about access. Control.

Understanding the game before others even realize they're playing it."

She listened. Learned. Adapted.

And by the time the night ended, she knew one thing for certain—

She had stepped into something she couldn't turn back from.

And she didn't want to.

# THE FIRST DEAL

A week later, she received her first real test.

A meeting was carefully arranged. A deal that needed closing.

She wasn't given instructions, just an outcome—**make it happen.**

And so, she did.

She walked into that boardroom, surrounded by men who had built empires, and she spoke with the kind of confidence that made them listen. She played the game not with arrogance, but with precision, knowing when to push and when to pull back.

By the time she left, the deal was done.

And when the message came through later that night—**"Well played."**—she allowed herself the smallest smile.

Because for the first time, she wasn't just chasing power.

She had it.

And this was only the beginning.

She had expected power to feel different.

Maybe like a surge of energy, an undeniable transformation. But as she sat alone in her apartment that night, replaying the events of the day, she realized power wasn't loud.

It was **quiet**.

It was in the way people looked at her now—not just with curiosity, but with calculation. It was in the way conversations shifted when she entered a room.

In this way, opportunities that once felt out of reach were now finding **her**.

She had spent years studying the game, observing the rules from the outside.

Now, she was inside.

And she wasn't going anywhere. **NAVIGATING THE NEW WORLD**

She moved carefully, deliberately.

Each meeting, each introduction was another step forward. She learned to read between the lines, to catch the subtleties in conversations that others might miss.

It wasn't just about money.

It was about **who you knew, who owed you favors, and who feared you enough to never cross you.**

And with every move, she understood something even more important—**power was not given. It was taken.**

She wasn't just taking a seat at the table.

She was **building her own.**

## A TEST OF LOYALTY

Not everyone welcomed her rise.

There were whispers—doubts about who she was, about where she had come from.

Some underestimated her. Others tried to **test** her.

One evening, at a gathering of high-profile investors, a man with salt-and-pepper hair and the kind of arrogance that came from old money leaned toward her with a knowing smirk.

"You're ambitious," he said, swirling the whiskey in his glass. "But tell me—do you actually know what you're doing? Or are you just good at pretending?"

She met his gaze without flinching. "Aren't we all pretending, in one way or another?"

His smirk faded slightly.

She leaned in. "The difference is, I don't have the luxury of underestimating people." A pause. "But you do."

Then she smiled.

And he said nothing.

Because they both knew—**she had already won.**

## A MESSAGE FROM THE PAST

She was moving forward. Climbing higher. Becoming the woman she had always envisioned herself to be.

But the past was never truly gone.

One night, after finalizing a deal that would cement her place among the elite, her phone buzzed with an unknown number.

She almost ignored it.

Until she saw the message.

**"Be careful. You're playing a dangerous game."**

Her stomach tightened.

There was no name, but she didn't need one.

She knew exactly who it was.

**Him.**

The man who had walked away.

The man who had left without answers.

And now, **he was back.**

She stared at the message, her grip tightening around the phone.

*"Be careful. You're playing a dangerous game."*

She had spent weeks trying to erase him from her mind, convincing herself that his absence was proof that their connection had been nothing more than an illusion.

But now, here he was. A ghost reappeared just when she was beginning to forget the sound of his voice.

Her fingers hovered over the keyboard.

She could ignore him.

Or she could respond.

And the truth was, she had never been good at walking away from unfinished business.

**Her Reply:** *You left. Why do you care now?*

She stared at the screen, waiting. Seconds stretched into minutes.

Then—three dots.

He was typing.

**His Response:** *Because I know what happens to people who reach too high.*

A warning. A threat. Or something else entirely.

She exhaled slowly, setting the phone down.

She wouldn't let him shake her.

Not now.

Not when she was this close to becoming everything she had worked for.

## THE WEIGHT OF POWER

In the days that followed, she buried herself deeper in this new world.

Every meeting, every calculated move brought her closer to the kind of influence she once only admired from afar.

But with power came scrutiny.

She could feel it—the way certain people watched her a little too closely. The way conversations shifted when she entered a room.

Some wanted to align with her. Others wanted to see her fail.

She had to be sharper, faster, untouchable.

And above all, she couldn't afford distractions.

Not even the kind that came with dark eyes and old scars.

## THE PAST COLLIDES WITH THE PRESENT

It was late when she saw him again.

A rooftop party, high above the city skyline. A celebration for a deal she had played a quiet but crucial role in securing.

The champagne flowed, and the air buzzed with laughter and ambition.

Then—**him.**

Standing across the terrace, watching her with an expression she couldn't read.

The crowd blurred around them, but he stayed sharp in focus. A reminder of everything she had tried to leave behind.

He didn't move toward her.

Didn't say a word.

But his presence alone was enough to unravel something inside her. And for the first time since she had stepped into this world, she felt it—

Doubt.

Because if he were back, it meant something was coming.

And she wasn't sure if she was ready for it.

She should have looked away. Should have ignored the way his presence made the air feel heavier, like the city itself had paused to acknowledge his return.

But she didn't.

Instead, she held his gaze, refusing to be the first to break.

If he had come back to shake her foundation, to remind her of who she used to be, he would fail. She wasn't that woman anymore.

Finally, he moved – slow, deliberate steps, closing the space between them like a force she couldn't escape.

"You've done well," he said, his voice low enough that only she could hear.

She took a sip of champagne, keeping her expression unreadable. "Did you come all this way just to say that?"

He studied her, his silence saying more than his words ever could. Then, finally—

"You think you have everything under control."

Her grip tightened around the glass, but she forced a calm smile. "I do."

He leaned in slightly, the heat of him too close, too familiar. "Then you don't understand the game you're playing."

She swallowed the retort that rose to her lips.

She had spent weeks mastering the rules, learning to navigate rooms filled with people who wielded wealth like a weapon. But he spoke like someone who had seen the game from a different angle—one she hadn't yet uncovered.

"I can handle myself," she said evenly.

A flicker of something—*concern? regret?*—passed through his eyes, gone before she could name it.

"Then prove it."

And just like that, he walked away, leaving her standing there, heart pounding, mind racing.

Prove it.

The words echoed in her head long after he had disappeared into the crowd.

And she would.

Not for him.

For herself.

## POWER ALWAYS COMES AT A COST

In the weeks that followed, she climbed higher.

More meetings. More alliances. More doors that once seemed permanently closed, now opening at the mere mention of her name.

But something had changed.

The higher she rose, the clearer it became—**power was not given without a price.**

The whispers grew louder. Deals became more dangerous. The choices she made carried consequences she couldn't yet see.

And then—

A message.

Delivered in an envelope slid beneath her door. No sender. No signature.

Just six words written in perfect, deliberate handwriting.

**"You're being watched. Choose wisely."**

A chill ran down her spine.

Because for the first time since stepping into this world—

She wasn't sure if she had stepped into it **or if she had been pulled in all along.**

# PART 2

## The Lady – Wealth, Power & The Private Jet Lifestyle

# Chapter 6: Reinvention

She had spent her whole life watching from the outside.

Studying the way the elite moved, how they spoke in half-truths and silent agreements. Influence wasn't just about money, but about **presence**—about knowing when to speak, when to listen, and when to make someone believe they needed you before they even realized it themselves.

Now, she wasn't watching anymore.

She was **inside**.

And this world, the one she had always admired from a distance, was no longer untouchable.

It was **hers to conquer.**

## THE FIRST REAL TEST

The invitation arrived in the form of a sleek, cream-colored card with gold lettering.

A gala hosted by one of the most powerful families in the city – old money, the kind that didn't just control corporations but shaped industries, economies, and futures.

She knew what this meant.

If she were invited, it wasn't just as a guest. It was a test.

They wanted to see if she belonged.

And she intended to prove that she did.

## BECOMING SOMEONE NEW

Reinvention wasn't about pretending to be someone else. It was about **elevating** who she already was.

Everything had to be calculated—her dress, her jewelry, the way she carried herself. Nothing too loud, nothing too desperate. Just enough power in her presence to command attention without asking for it.

By the time she stepped into the ballroom, every detail had been perfected.

She didn't just look like she belonged.

She felt it.

## PLAYING THE GAME

Power wasn't in grand gestures. It was in the subtle things—the way conversations were held in quiet corners, the way alliances were made over a sip of champagne rather than in boardrooms.

She moved carefully, reading the room as if it were a chessboard.

A nod here. A smile there. A carefully placed comment that hinted at knowledge she wasn't supposed to have.

People noticed.

By the end of the night, she wasn't just another guest.

She was **a wife, sister, and mum. More than a player, she was the heart and soul. But she didn't want to reveal her vulnerable side, and for her family, she played along as a player.**

## A WARNING FROM THE PAST

She was sipping her drink when a familiar voice cut through the noise.

"I see you've adapted well."

She turned.

**Him.**

Standing just close enough that no one else could hear.

She took her time before answering. "I had a good teacher."

His lips curled slightly, but there was something unreadable in his gaze.

Something that sent a slow chill down her spine.

"You think you understand this world now."

She held his stare. "I do."

A beat of silence.

Then—**"No. You only think you do."**

She hated how those words settled in her chest, heavy and foreboding.

Because she knew he wasn't just talking about society.

He was talking about the **game beneath the game.**

The one she wasn't supposed to see yet.

And suddenly, she wondered—

Was she really in control?

Or had she just walked into something far bigger than she had ever imagined?

She refused to let his words shake her.

For weeks, she had moved through this world with precision, learning the unspoken rules and mastering the art of influence. She had stepped into high society not as an outsider begging for acceptance but as someone who **belonged.**

And yet, he stood before her now, looking at her as if she were still playing a game she didn't fully understand.

"You're always so sure of yourself," she said, swirling the last of her champagne in her glass. "But tell me—what exactly am I missing?"

His gaze flickered, almost as if he were debating whether to tell her. Then, he leaned in slightly, his voice low.

"You think power is about who you know." A pause. "But real power is about what you know—and what you're willing to do with it." The weight of his words settled in her chest.

This wasn't a compliment. It was a challenge. A warning.

Before she could respond, someone called her name. A woman—elegant, older, the kind whose wealth had been passed down through generations rather than earned.

His attention shifted, just for a moment, but it was enough.

By the time she looked back at him, he was already walking away.

And she hated the way it felt like **she was the one being left behind this time.**

## POWER COMES WITH A PRICE

In the days that followed, she threw herself deeper into the world she was building.

Meetings with investors. Strategic alliances with people who had more influence than she had ever imagined. Every step forward was another layer of protection, another way to ensure that no one—**not even him could** make her doubt herself again.

But the more she learned, the more she realized something unsettling.

This world wasn't just about wealth.

It was about **control**.

And some people would do anything to keep it.

## THE FIRST REAL THREAT

It came in the form of a message, much like before.

No name. No signature.

Just a simple sentence typed with cold precision:

**"Be careful where you step. Not every door should be opened."**

She stared at the words, her heart pounding.

This wasn't just about high society anymore.

Someone was watching.

Someone didn't want her getting too close.

And for the first time since she had stepped into this world—

She wondered if she was being invited in.

Or if she was being **warned away.**

The message sat on her screen like a challenge.

*"Be careful where you step. Not every door should be opened."*

She had spent weeks proving she belonged, moving through circles once closed to her, forging connections that made her indispensable. But this? This was different.

This wasn't intriguing.

This was **a warning.**

She exhaled slowly, locking her phone and setting it aside. Fear was a luxury she couldn't afford.

If someone wanted her to back off, that meant she was getting close to something important.

And she had never been one to walk away from an opportunity.

## A LESSON IN POWER

The next night, she attended another gathering—this time, smaller and more private. It was the kind where real deals happened behind closed doors, far from the spectacle of high society galas.

She had been invited by a man she had met at the gala, a venture capitalist whose name carried weight in every financial circle that mattered.

"You're making people nervous," he said, pouring her a drink as they stood in the shadows of the rooftop terrace. "They don't like it when someone rises too quickly."

She took the glass but didn't drink. "Should I be worried?"

He smirked. "Not if you're smart."

She met his gaze. "And if I'm not?"

The smirk faded. "Then you'll disappear like the others."

A slow chill ran down her spine, but she kept her expression steady.

"Good thing I'm smart, then."

He studied her for a long moment before clinking his glass lightly against hers.

"Then welcome to the real game."

## THE REALIZATION

That night, she understood something she hadn't understood before.

It wasn't enough to **enter** this world.

She had to survive it.

She had thought reinvention was about changing how people saw her. About proving she belonged.

But now, she realized—it wasn't just about fitting in.

It was about **power.**

And power didn't come from acceptance.

It came from making sure no one could **push you out.**

Whatever was waiting on the other side of that warning, she was ready.

Because she hadn't come this far just to be told which doors she could or couldn't open.

She was here to **own the entire house.**

Power had a rhythm. A flow.

She had learned to navigate it – when to push, when to hold back, when to let others believe they were leading while she pulled the strings from the shadows. But something had shifted.

The message. The warning. The quiet way conversations paused when she walked into a room.

She was being watched.

The question wasn't *who.*

It was *why.*

# A DANGEROUS INVITATION

Days later, she received another invitation.

This one wasn't printed on elegant cardstock or delivered with a knowing smile.

It was a plain white envelope slipped under her door.

Inside, a single note.

**"Midnight. The lounge on Fifth. No questions."**

She knew the place—exclusive, expensive, the kind where deals were made over whispered conversations and fortunes changed hands with a signature.

It wasn't an invitation.

It was a summons.

She could ignore it.

Or she could find out exactly who was pulling the strings behind the curtain.

She went.

# A NEW PLAYER ENTERS

The lounge was dimly lit, the scent of expensive cigars and aged whiskey lingering in the air.

She spotted him immediately.

A man she had never met, but one whose presence **commanded** the room. Older, sharp-eyed, with the kind of quiet authority that came from **owning things other people didn't even know existed.**

He gestured to the seat across from him.

She sat.

A server poured them both a drink.

He lifted his glass. "To your success."

She didn't move. "You don't even know me."

A slight smile. "But I know what you're becoming."

She met his gaze, unblinking. "And what's that?"

He swirled the liquid in his glass before answering.

"Someone worth watching."

A pause.

Then—"**But tell me... do you understand what happens when too many people start watching?**"

She didn't flinch.

Because she did.

It meant she was getting too close to something.

Something people didn't want her to see.

And if that were the case, she had only one choice.

**Look harder.**

She didn't break eye contact.

There was a test in his words, a quiet challenge disguised as a warning.

*"Do you understand what happens when too many people start watching?"*

She took a slow sip of her drink before answering. "I suppose that depends on who's watching."

His smile was slight but knowing. "Smart answer."

She leaned forward slightly. "But not the one you were looking for, was it?"

He chuckled. "No, but it tells me exactly what I needed to know."

She arched an eyebrow, waiting.

He set his glass down. "You're moving fast. Too fast."

She didn't flinch. "I didn't realize there was a speed limit."

"There isn't," he admitted. "But there are boundaries. Unwritten rules. You've managed to skip a few steps most people spend years navigating." He studied her. "That makes you valuable. It also makes you dangerous."

"Dangerous to whom?"

His expression didn't change. "To the people who built this world before you got here."

Silence stretched between them.

She had known this moment would come.

For weeks, she had felt it — the shift in the way people looked at her, the weight of whispers that never quite reached her ears.

She had been allowed in.

But now, she had to prove she **belonged**.

"I assume you didn't bring me here just to warn me," she said smoothly.

"No," he admitted. "I brought you here to offer you a choice."

She didn't respond, waiting.

"You can keep playing the game as you are, taking calculated risks, hoping the right doors open for you," he leaned back. "Or you can learn how to **own** the game."

Her pulse quickened, but she kept her expression neutral.

"And how would I do that?"

His lips curved slightly. "By understanding where the real power lies."

She tilted her head. "And where is that?"

He reached into his pocket and slid a sleek black card across the table.

No name. No logo. Just a single line of embossed text.

**"The future isn't built on paper. It's built on code."** She lifted the card, running her thumb over the letters.

A statement. A clue.

And an invitation.

He watched her carefully. "Do you want to stop being watched?"

A pause.

"Then learn how to disappear."

The message was clear.

Power wasn't just about money anymore.

It was about something bigger.

Something digital.

Something **borderless**.

And if she wanted to survive in this world, she needed to understand it.

Because the next step in her reinvention wasn't just about influence.

It was about **control.**

# Chapter 7: The Crypto Connection

Power was shifting.

Not just in boardrooms, not just in old money circles.

It was happening in the digital space—unseen by those who still clung to traditional wealth. The world was changing, and those who understood the new language of money weren't just growing rich.

They were **rewriting the rules.**

And now, she was about to learn how.

## THE FIRST LESSON

She traced the embossed letters on the black card he had given her.

*"The future isn't built on paper. It's built on code."*

The words lingered in her mind, a riddle she intended to solve.

A few nights later, she found herself in an unfamiliar part of the city, standing in front of an unmarked building. There were no signs, no obvious security, just a single door with a biometric scanner.

She pressed the card against it. A faint beep. The door unlocked.

Inside, the atmosphere was nothing like the elite galas she had grown accustomed to. The air was charged, humming with quiet conversations and the glow of screens. The people here weren't draped in luxury—they were draped in **information.**

No one acknowledged her at first.

Then, a voice from the shadows.

"You made it."

She turned.

**Him.**

Not the man from the gala, but someone younger and sharper—the kind of person who didn't exist in corporate databases but could wipe them clean with a few keystrokes.

He smirked. "Welcome to the real economy."

## THE DIGITAL UNDERGROUND

She had thought she understood wealth. She had spent months studying power, learning how influence moved.

But this? This was something else entirely.

There were no physical assets here. No luxury skyscrapers, no banks controlling the flow of money.

Here, money **moved without borders.**

It wasn't held. It was **transferred. Traded. Multiplied.**

Bitcoin. Ethereum. DeFi. Smart contracts. Anonymous wallets are moving millions in seconds.

She listened, absorbing everything.

"Control isn't about owning something anymore," her guide explained. "It's about controlling access."

She watched as he flipped his screen toward her, showing an account balance that didn't just have numbers.

It had **power.**

"This is how the world is really run now," he said. "And if you're smart enough, fast enough—you'll never have to answer to anyone again."

Her pulse quickened.

This was more than money.

This was **freedom.**

And for the first time, she understood why people feared those who truly controlled it.

Because **wealth was no longer something you could see.**

It was something you could **hide.**

And now, she was ready to learn exactly how.

She had always thought of wealth as tangible—real estate, luxury cars, and hefty bank accounts. But here, in this dimly lit room filled with glowing screens and quiet conversations, she saw a different kind of wealth.

One that **moved in silence.**

One that **couldn't be traced.**

One that **belonged to those who understood the game before the world even realized it was being played.**

## A NEW TYPE OF POWER

She spent hours listening and learning.

They spoke in codes—**NFTs, staking, decentralized exchanges, liquidity pools.** Terms that had never been part of the world she had once admired, but here, they were everything.

Modern warfare is ancient warfare; both combined with epic warfare is **DIGITAL WARFARE.**

She quickly realized the truth:

**Crypto wasn't just about making money.**

It was about **hiding it. Multiplying it. Controlling it.**

"Most people still think wealth means having a name on a building," one of them said, scrolling through a live market feed. "But the smartest people? They don't want to be seen at all."

She leaned in. "And how do you do that?"

The man smirked, clicking on an anonymous digital wallet. "By making sure the money moves so fast, no one can catch it."

She watched as he executed a series of trades in seconds, flipping digital assets between wallets, exchanges, and private holdings. The numbers changed instantly, value shifting across borders without a single government having a say in it.

It was **power**, but not the kind she had known before.

It was the kind of power that **didn't answer to anyone.**

## THE FIRST MOVE

They tested her.

Not with questions, but with opportunity.

"Show us what you've learned," one of them said, sliding a laptop toward her.

She glanced at the screen – a decentralized exchange, a volatile market, thousands of trades happening every second.

It was a risk.

But she had built her entire life on knowing when to take one.

Her fingers moved over the keyboard, analyzing trends, executing trades, shifting assets.

Five minutes later, she leaned back.

The screen showed the results.

A profit. A significant one.

The group exchanged looks. One of them nodded. "She's in." She exhaled, steadying herself.

She had stepped into a new world.

And she had **already proved she belonged.**

# THE WARNING THAT CAME TOO LATE

Later that night, as she walked back into the quiet of her apartment, her phone buzzed.

**Unknown Number:** *You're getting reckless.*

She stared at the message, her heartbeat slowing.

**Unknown Number:** *You don't know who you're dealing with.*

She didn't need to ask who it was.

She already knew.

**Him.**

The one who had left. The one who had warned her before.

The one who, even now, was still watching.

She typed her response slowly, deliberately.

**Me:** *I know exactly what I'm doing.*

A pause.

Then, three dots.

He was typing.

Her breath caught as the reply appeared.

**Him:** *Then you're in more danger than you realize.*

She locked the screen and set the phone down.

She wasn't turning back.

Not now. Not ever.

She told herself she wouldn't let his words get to her.

*"Then you're in more danger than you realize."*

It was just another warning. Another attempt to make her doubt herself.

But doubt wasn't an option anymore.

She had stepped too far into this world to back out now.

And what if there was danger?

She would learn how to **control it** before it could control her.

## THE FIRST REAL THREAT

The next morning, she woke up to another message.

Different number. Same unsettling tone.

**Unknown:** *Some things aren't meant to be found.*

No name. No explanation.

Just a reminder that someone was watching her every move.

She gripped the phone tightly, her mind racing.

This wasn't just about money anymore.

She was getting too close to something–something people didn't want her to see.

And that meant she had a choice.

Step back.

Or go deeper.

She already knew what she was going to do.

## A MEETING IN THE SHADOWS

That night, she returned to the underground crypto hub.

The man who had introduced her to this world—**Kade**, as she had learned—was waiting.

"Your name's coming up in the wrong conversations," he said, leaning against a desk filled with open trading screens.

She crossed her arms. "Whose conversations?"

He didn't answer right away. Instead, he slid a tablet across the table.

She looked down. A transaction history—anonymous accounts, massive amounts of money being moved in patterns that didn't make sense.

Except they did.

Because these weren't trades.

These were **laundering patterns.**

One of the accounts—buried beneath layers of digital obfuscation—was associated with a name she **recognized.**

Her pulse quickened.

She glanced back at Kade. "How did you get this?"

His expression remained unreadable. "Does it matter?"

She inhaled slowly. "And why are you showing me?"

"Because now you're part of it," he said simply. "Whether you meant to be or not."

A chill ran down her spine. She had come here for wealth. For power.

But she was beginning to realize—**some doors, once opened, could never be closed.**

And this one?

She had just stepped straight through it.

She should have walked away.

She should have pretended she hadn't seen the numbers, the names, the quiet transactions moving beneath the surface of the digital world.

But she wasn't wired that way.

She had spent too long chasing power, too long learning the rules to stop now.

So instead of fear, she felt something else.

**Determination.**

If she were part of this game, then she needed to know exactly what she was playing.

And who was playing against her?

# A DANGEROUS DISCOVERY

She spent the next few days buried in research.

Hidden forums. Private servers. Blockchain records that had been wiped clean – but nothing was ever truly erased.

The deeper she dug, the clearer the pattern became.

Someone was using crypto to move **massive** amounts of money – fast, untraceable, across borders.

And the name buried beneath layers of false identities?

It was someone **she had met before.**

Someone from high society.

Someone powerful enough to make problems disappear.

Her stomach tightened.

This wasn't just about financial freedom anymore.

This was about something **far bigger.**

And she had just **linked herself to it.**

# THE WARNING SHE COULDN'T IGNORE

She was sitting in her apartment, her laptop screen glowing in the dim light, when the notification popped up.

**Anonymous Message:** *You should stop looking.*

Her breath stilled.

It wasn't a suggestion.

It was a **command.**

A heartbeat later, another message.

**Anonymous Message:** *People disappear for less.*

Her pulse pounded in her ears.

She glanced toward her door, half expecting someone to already be there.

But she wasn't the same woman she had been months ago.

She wasn't going to be scared off by a few words on a screen.

So instead of closing her laptop, she opened a secure channel.

And she sent a message of her own.

**Me:** *Then maybe they should be more careful about what they leave behind.*

A risk. A challenge.

She had no idea if she had just made a mistake.

But one thing was certain.

If they thought she would back down, they were **dead wrong.**

The message was sent.

She sat back, heart pounding, watching the screen as if it might reveal something more.

But nothing came.

No reply. No further warning.

Just silence.

The kind that wasn't comforting—but **calculated**.

Someone was deciding what to do with her.

She had their attention now.

The question was—**what would they do next?**

## THE TRAP SHE DIDN'T SEE COMING

The invitation arrived two days later.

Not through encrypted messages or anonymous threats—this time, it was **elegant.**

A formal event. A high society fundraiser for "philanthropic ventures."

She almost laughed at the irony.

A room full of men who moved money in places no one could trace, gathering under the pretense of giving it away.

She should have said no.

She should have seen it for what it was—**a test. A setup.**

But she wasn't the kind of woman who ran from confrontation.

So, she went.

## A GAME OF MASKS

The venue was stunning.

Crystal chandeliers, gold-trimmed décor, the kind of place where conversations were polite on the surface and **ruthless underneath.**

She moved through the crowd, nodding at familiar faces, feeling the weight of **being watched.**

Then, she saw him.

Not the anonymous threats. Not the traders from the digital underground.

But **the man whose name had been buried in those blockchain transactions.**

The one she had traced.

And the moment he turned toward her, glass of champagne in hand, expression unreadable, she knew.

He wasn't surprised to see her.

He had **expected** her to come.

And that meant **she had just walked straight into their game.**

## A DANGEROUS CONVERSATION

He approached her first.

"Impressive," he murmured, offering a polite smile as he clinked his glass lightly against hers.

She met his gaze without flinching. "What is?"

"The way you find things that aren't meant to be found."

Her fingers tightened around the stem of her glass.

"So, tell me," he continued, tilting his head slightly. "Did you come here tonight to ask questions?"

She took a slow sip of champagne, masking the sharp edge of adrenaline in her veins.

"Would you answer them if I did?"

His smile didn't fade, but something in his eyes shifted – just slightly.

"No," he said simply.

A heartbeat passed.

"Then I guess I'm just here for the drinks," she replied smoothly.

For a moment, neither of them moved.

Then, he leaned in, his voice just low enough for her alone.

"You're smart," he said. "So be smarter than this."

She exhaled slowly. "And if I'm not?"

His smile returned.

"Then you won't have to worry about what happens next."

A warning. A promise.

And the moment he walked away, disappearing into the crowd, she knew—

She was **in too deep.**

But it was **too late to stop now.**

She watched as he disappeared into the crowd, his words lingering like smoke in the air.

*"Then you won't have to worry about what happens next."*

A warning wrapped in a smile.

She should have been afraid. Maybe she was.

But fear wasn't going to stop her.

Not when she was this close to **understanding the real game.**

## THE COST OF KNOWLEDGE

By the time she left the event, the city felt different.

The streets were the same. The skyline remains unchanged. But the way she **moved** through it had shifted.

She wasn't just an outsider looking in anymore.

She had been **noticed.**

And that meant one thing—**she was a threat.**

She needed to act before someone acted against her.

# A HIDDEN MEETING

Kade wasn't surprised when she showed up at the underground hub.

"I was wondering how long it'd take before you came looking for answers," he said, shutting his laptop.

She dropped her bag onto the table, eyes sharp. "You knew."

He didn't deny it.

"You don't get this far without making enemies," he said. "You're disrupting something bigger than you realize."

She crossed her arms. "Then tell me what I don't see." He exhaled, studying her before finally speaking.

"They're not just moving money. They're **controlling** it."

She frowned. "How?"

"Through digital ledgers, shadow networks. The kind of transactions that governments can't regulate because they don't even know they exist." He leaned back. "That's what you stepped into. Not just wealth—**power over the entire system.**"

Her stomach tightened.

This wasn't about laundering money or hiding assets.

It was about **rewriting the way money worked altogether.**

And she had just stumbled into the middle of it.

## A LINE SHE COULDN'T CROSS—YET

She inhaled deeply, absorbing what this meant.

If she kept going, she wouldn't just be playing with digital assets.

She'd be stepping into **the architecture of power itself.**

There would be no way to stay neutral.

She would have to choose a side.

And once she did, **there would be no turning back.**

She met Kade's gaze. "Who's really running this?"

He hesitated.

Then, finally—

"People you don't want to owe favors to."

She clenched her jaw.

She had spent her life making the right alliances, learning to navigate rooms full of people who thought they controlled everything.

But now, she wasn't sure if she had been playing the game—**or if the game had been playing her all along.**

She had spent her whole life making moves, positioning herself where she needed to be.

But now, for the first time, she wasn't sure if she was moving toward power—**or being pulled deeper into someone else's game.**

Kade's words echoed in her mind.

*"People you don't want to owe favors to."*

She had always believed that money was the ultimate advantage.

But this?

This was about **control.**

And control had a price.

## A SILENT THREAT

Two days passed.

She stayed quiet, watching, waiting – seeing if anything would happen after the gala, after her conversation with Kade.

Then, it did.

It wasn't a message this time.

No texts, no warnings, no cryptic threats.

Just **an account missing.**

One of her crypto wallets – one she had carefully built, one that had grown significantly in value – was gone.

Not hacked. Not drained.

Just **erased.**

As if it had never existed.

She stared at the empty screen, a slow wave of realization washing over her.

They weren't sending messages anymore.

They were showing her what they could do.

## A DANGEROUS OFFER

That night, she received a call.

Unknown number.

She answered, anyway.

A smooth voice filled the line. Male. Calm. Calculated.

"We haven't met," he said. "But I think it's time we do."

She kept her voice steady. "And who's that?"

A pause. Then—

"Because you're in deeper than you think. And I'd hate for you to learn that the hard way."

Her grip tightened around the phone.

"I don't scare easily," she said.

A quiet chuckle. "Then you're exactly the kind of person we're looking for."

The line went dead.

No location. No details.

Just an expectation that she would know how to find them.

And the worst part?

She already did.

# A CHOICE THAT WASN'T REALLY A CHOICE

She could walk away now.

Pretend she had never traced those transactions, never followed the money, never asked the wrong questions.

Or—

She could go deeper.

Step into the rooms where real power was traded.

The kind of power that wasn't just about **wealth.**

But about **who held the keys to the system itself.**

And she had spent too long fighting for a seat at the table to turn back now.

So, the next night, she got dressed.

And she went to meet them.

Whatever *they* were.

Whatever *they* wanted.

And whatever *they* thought she was ready for.

# Chapter 8: Duality of Self

She had always believed she could separate the past from the present.

That ambition could erase old wounds. That power could drown out the echoes of emotions she had long buried.

But now, standing at the threshold of a world that promised **everything**—wealth, influence, untouchable control—she felt the past creeping back in.

A quiet reminder that she hadn't always been this version of herself.

And that maybe, just maybe, a part of her never would be.

## THE MEETING THAT CHANGED EVERYTHING

She arrived at the location sent to her – a penthouse suite, high above the city, where the skyline looked small and distant, as if it belonged to someone else entirely.

Inside, the air was thick with quiet conversations and veiled negotiations.

These weren't the wealthy elites she had learned to navigate.

They were something else.

**The Architects of Power.**

And as she was led into a private room, she realized something unsettling.

They had been watching her long before she started watching them.

## THE OFFER

A man sat across from her. The same voice from the call—smooth, controlled, dangerous in its patience.

"You've proven yourself," he said, pouring a drink neither of them touched.

"Most people who start pulling at threads don't make it this far."

She kept her expression neutral. "And what happens to the ones who do?"

He smiled slightly. "They get choices."

He slid a folder across the table.

Inside—her own name. Her own **entire** financial footprint. Accounts, trades, investments, even details she hadn't told anyone.

Proof that she wasn't in control.

That **they** were.

"This is everything you've built," he said simply. "And with one decision, it can all disappear."

She met his gaze, unblinking. "Or?"

His smile didn't fade.

"Or you can be part of something much bigger."

## THE PAST VS. THE FUTURE

She exhaled slowly, fingers tracing the edges of the folder.

This was what she had wanted, wasn't it?

To stop being the one chasing power and start being the one **wielding it**.

But somewhere in the back of her mind, a different voice whispered.

**His voice.**

*"You think you have control, but you don't even see the real game."*

She had spent months convincing herself he was wrong.

That she was choosing this life, shaping it on her terms.

But looking at the folder, at the proof that they had been **ten steps ahead of her all along—**

She felt something she hadn't felt in a long time.

**Doubt.**

Because for the first time since she had started this journey, she wasn't sure if she was still climbing to the top.

Or if she had just **become another piece on their board.**

And worse—

If she even cared.

She stared at the folder.

Her name. Her records. Her entire financial empire lay out before her as if it were nothing more than a file to be handled, controlled, erased, or expanded, binding on what *they* decided.

She had fought to build this.

Yet here it was, **already in someone else's hands.**

A cold realization settled over her.

Maybe she had never truly been in control.

Maybe she had only been **allowed** to believe she was.

## THE QUESTION THAT WOULD DEFINE EVERYTHING

The man across from her watched in silence, letting her absorb what this moment really meant.

Then, finally—

"Do you know why you're here?" he asked.

Her jaw tightened. "Because I made too much noise." His lips curved slightly. "No. Because you showed promise."

A pause.

"You think we would have let you get this far if we didn't want you here?"

The weight of his words settled deep in her chest.

She had spent so long believing she was **outsmarting the system**—climbing higher, pushing boundaries, proving she belonged.

But what if she had never really been fighting her way in?

What if she had been **guided here all along?**

## PAST VS. PRESENT

A part of her wanted to walk away.

She wanted to reclaim whatever was left of the person she had once been before wealth, power, and strategy had reshaped her into someone unrecognizable.

But another part—the part that had **always** wanted more—whispered:

*"You didn't come this far just to stop now."*

That voice was louder.

It had always been louder.

And she wasn't sure if she still wanted to fight it.

Or if she had already lost to it completely.

# THE DECISION THAT WASN'T REALLY A DECISION

She lifted her gaze to the man in front of her.

"I suppose this is the part where I ask what you want from me."

He smirked.

"No," he said simply. "This is the part where you tell us how far you're willing to go."

Her pulse quickened.

Not from fear.

From **knowing.**

Because deep down, she already had her answer.

She just wasn't sure if it was **her** answer.

Or the answer they had **always known she would give.**

She knew the answer before she even opened her mouth.

But something in her hesitated.

Not out of fear. Not even out of doubt.

But because she could feel it—**the weight of the moment.**

This wasn't just another deal.

It wasn't just another step forward.

This was the point of no return.

Once she said yes, she wasn't just part of the game.

She was **owned by it.**

**THE OFFER SEALED IN SILENCE** The man across from her didn't push.

He didn't need to.

They both knew she wasn't walking away.

Instead of answering, she reached for her glass, taking a slow sip of the untouched drink between them.

She let the silence stretch.

Let the moment settle.

Then, finally, she set the glass down.

A quiet acceptance.

The only answer they needed.

The man smiled.

"Good," he said, leaning back. "Now let's begin."

And just like that—

The choice was made.

Or maybe, it had never really been a choice at all.

## THE WEIGHT OF POWER

She left the penthouse that night feeling both **lighter and heavier at the same time.**

Lighter because she had **shed the last remnants of hesitation.**

Heavier because she had just **become something she could never undo.**

She had spent months shaping herself into this version of who she wanted to be.

But now, standing on the edge of true power, she couldn't shake one thought—Was this still her?

Or had she been rewritten by the very thing she once thought she controlled?

The past whispered to her, reminding her of **who she used to be.**

The present drowned it out, pulling her toward **who she was becoming.**

And the future?

The future no longer belonged to her alone.

She had **given herself to it.**

And she wasn't sure if she had gained everything—

Or if she had just lost **the last piece of herself.**

# Chapter 9: Love vs. Control

Power changed everything.

The way people looked at her. The way they spoke to her.

And, most importantly, **the way they loved her.**

If love were even real in this world.

Because here, nothing was given freely.

Everything had a cost.

Even affection.

Even desire.

Even *him*.

## A NEW PLAYER IN THE GAME

It started like all things do—calculated, intentional, a move that didn't seem like one.

His name was Abi.

Wealthy. Influential. Unpredictable.

He wasn't like the others.

He didn't chase. He didn't flatter.

He simply **existed in her orbit**, watching, waiting—like he already knew they were inevitable.

And maybe they were.

Because from the moment she met him, she felt it—
**the tension, the pull.**

The unspoken question hangs between them.

Was he drawn to *her*?

Or to the **power she now carried?**

## THE GAME OF ATTRACTION

Their interactions were slow and deliberate.

A glance across a crowded room. A conversation filled with words that meant one thing on the surface and something else entirely underneath.

He was **measured.**

She was **guarded.**

Neither was willing to give the other the upper hand.

But power had its own gravity.

And the more they resisted, the closer they got.

Until one night—

It snapped.

## A KISS THAT MEANT MORE

It wasn't planned.

It wasn't a calculated move.

It just *happened.*

A stolen moment in the quiet of a rooftop, the city glowing below them.

One second, they were standing apart.

The next, **his lips were on hers.**

Heat. Electricity. A collision of control and surrender.

She didn't stop him.

Didn't *want* to stop him.

Because for the first time in a long time, she wasn't thinking about power plays or strategy.

She was just *feeling*.

But the second it ended, reality came crashing back.

Because the question still remained.

Did he want *her*?

Or was this just another way to **own a piece of her world?**

And worse—

Did she even care?

She should have walked away.

A single kiss shouldn't have meant anything.

She had kissed men before—some out of passion, some out of strategy, some just to prove she could.

But **this-this** wasn't simple.

Because when Abi pulled away, there was no triumph in his eyes. No smirk.

No indication that he had just **won something.**

Instead, he looked at her as if he were **waiting for her reaction.**

As if he knew she was already searching for the angle.

And that was the problem.

She didn't know if there **was** an angle.

Or if this was the first thing in a long time that was **real.**

## THE RULES OF ENGAGEMENT

The days that followed were filled with tension.

Not avoidance—because neither of them was a coward—but something more dangerous.

A **push and pull.**

A dance between what was **business** and what was **personal.**

Meetings turned into quiet drinks. Conversations held weight, but they never acknowledged them.

And then there were the nights.

The stolen moments behind closed doors, where the lines blurred further—where he touched her like she was his to claim, and she let him, knowing full well that **no one in this world ever truly belonged to anyone.**

## A DANGEROUS QUESTION

One evening, after yet another deal had been sealed, another layer of trust built, she found herself alone with him again.

The city stretched below them, glittering with wealth, with power.

With **lies.** Damned lies. Statistics.

She leaned against the railing, swirling her drink. "Tell me something."

He turned to her, waiting.

"Is this just another negotiation?" she asked, her voice calm, unreadable. "Another deal to be made?"

She expected him to evade, to smirk, to give her a **non-answer**.

But instead, he surprised her.

He stepped closer, so close that the space between them became insignificant.

"Would it change anything if it were?"

She inhaled sharply.

Because for the first time, she didn't know.

Would it?

She had built herself into someone untouchable. Someone who could walk away from anything without regret.

But standing here, with **him**, she wasn't sure if she was playing the game anymore—

Or if, for the first time, **she was the one being played.**

She should have answered him.

Should have said something sharp, something indifferent, something that would put them **back in control**—back in familiar territory where neither of them owed the other anything.

But she didn't.

Because the truth was, she didn't know the answer.

And that terrified her.

So instead, she did what she had always done.

She deflected.

She turned away, taking a slow sip of her drink. "You're asking the wrong question, Abi," he didn't push.

Didn't demand clarity.

He just watched her, waiting.

Because they both knew—

If she had to **ask** whether this was real, then maybe it wasn't.

Maybe it never had been. **THE COST OF VULNERABILITY.**

That night, she couldn't sleep.

It wasn't the deals she had made or the risks she had taken that kept her awake.

It was **him.**

The way he looked at her, like he saw past the armor she had spent years building. The way he touched her, like he wasn't trying to claim her, but trying to **understand** her.

It unsettled her.

Because power, she understood. Strategy, she could control.

But **this?**

This was dangerous in a way nothing else had ever been.

Because if she let herself believe it was real—

Then she had something to lose.

And she had spent too long making sure **she had nothing to lose.**

## A LINE DRAWN IN THE SAND

The next time they saw each other, she was ready.

She had made her choice.

And she wasn't going to let herself slip.

He greeted her as if nothing had changed, but she saw the shift in his eyes the moment she spoke.

"This—" she gestured between them, keeping her voice steady—"can't happen."

A flicker of something crossed his face. Disappointment? Amusement? It was gone before she could name it.

"Why not?"

She exhaled. "Because I don't do this."

He studied her for a long moment.

Then, his voice dropped just slightly. "You don't do *what?*"

She swallowed. "Uncertainty."

A slow smile. "No," he said. "You don't do *things you can't control.*"

Her chest tightened.

Because he was right.

And they both knew it.

## WALKING AWAY

She left before he could say anything else.

Because if he did – if he gave her a reason to stay –

She wasn't sure she would be strong enough to leave.

And weakness?

That wasn't something she could afford.

Not now.

Not ever.

But as she walked away, the truth settled deep in her bones.

She could shut him out.

She could end this before it became a liability.

But it was already too late.

Because if she had truly been in control—

She wouldn't have had to **convince herself** to walk away.

She simply **would have.**

# Chapter 10: The Price of Success

Success was supposed to feel like victory.

But standing at the top, looking down at everything she had built, she realized **it felt more like survival.**

She had done everything right.

Played the game better than anyone expected.

And now, she was exactly where she had always wanted to be.

**Untouchable.**

**Unstoppable.**

**Alone.**

## THE COST OF POWER

The higher she climbed, the fewer people she could trust.

Allies turned into competitors.

Smiles masked quiet threats.

And even in the most exclusive rooms, surrounded by the wealthiest and most powerful, she felt something creeping in at the edges.

**Paranoia.**

Because in this world, no one stays on top forever.

And if she wasn't careful, she wouldn't just fall—**they would make sure she was erased.**

## A KNIFE IN THE DARK

The first real betrayal didn't come from an enemy.

It came from someone she had trusted.

A deal she had spent months orchestrating—sabotaged at the last moment.

A partnership dissolved, assets frozen, an entire empire suddenly **at risk.**

She had expected challenges.

What she hadn't expected **was for the attack to come from within.**

She stared at the documents before her, her mind calculating every possible move.

Whoever had done this didn't just want to take what she had.

They wanted to **break her.**

And she would rather **burn it all to the ground** than let that happen. She is indeed the wildfire.

## THE FINAL SACRIFICE

She had spent so long believing success meant **winning at any cost.**

That power was the only thing that mattered.

But now, as she prepared to strike back—**to remind them who they were dealing with**—she felt something else.

A question she couldn't shake.

Was this **all** there was?

Had she traded too much of herself to get here?

Or worse—had she **always known this was the price** and chosen to pay it anyway?

Because power had given her everything.

Except for the one thing it couldn't buy.

**Peace.**

She had always known power came at a cost.

She hadn't realized **how much of herself she would have to give up to keep it.**

There was no turning back now.

Her empire was under attack.

And if she wanted to stay on top, she had to **remind them all why she was here in the first place.**

# THE ART OF RETALIATION

She didn't lash out.

Didn't panic.

She **calculated.**

Because the real game wasn't about reacting – it was about **controlling the response.**

Within hours, she had answers.

The betrayal had come from someone close.

Someone who had stood beside her, smiled in her face, and then made the first move against her.

And that was their mistake.

They had forgotten **who they were dealing with.**

## POWER IS NOT GIVEN—IT'S TAKEN

The counterattack was swift.

She pulled strings they didn't even know existed.

Turned their allies against them.

Cut off their resources before they even knew what was happening.

It was already over by the time they realized what she had done.

They weren't just **removed from the board—**

**They were erased.**

And just like that, she had proven what she had always known:

**There was no room for weakness at the top.**

## A LIFE THAT NO LONGER FELT LIKE HERS

She won.

Of course, she won.

But when the dust settled and her empire was safe again, she felt **the emptiness.**

There was no satisfaction.

No celebration.

Just **another battle survived.**

And another reminder that the higher she climbed, the lonelier it became.

The ones she trusted were gone.

The ones she loved – if she had ever really loved – had been left behind.

All that remained was **power.** And for the first time, she wondered—

Was that ever really enough?

Or had she built something she could never escape from?

A **prison disguised as a throne.**

And worse—

Had she **locked herself inside?**

Victory had never felt this hollow.

She had won. Again.

But success wasn't a celebration anymore.

It was **a cycle** – one she couldn't break.

Because the second you stopped fighting in this world, someone else was ready to **take your place.**

And she had worked too hard to be erased.

# THE GHOSTS OF WHO SHE USED TO BE

She stood at the window of her penthouse, staring at the city below.

The view was the same.

But **she wasn't.**

She thought about the girl she used to be – the one who believed power would fill the empty spaces inside her.

She had spent years climbing, **becoming untouchable.**

Now, she had everything she had ever wanted.

And yet—

She felt **nothing.**

# A CALL THAT CHANGED EVERYTHING

Her phone buzzed.

An **unknown number.**

She almost ignored it.

Then—**instinct.**

She answered.

A pause.

Then, a voice she hadn't expected.

**Adi**

"It's done," he said.

No greeting. No warmth. Just those two words, weighted with meaning.

She exhaled. "I know."

Silence stretched between them.

Then—

"Are you happy?"

Her fingers tightened around the phone.

She could have lied.

She could have said, **Yes. This is precisely what I wanted.**

But for once, **she didn't have an answer.**

## TRAPPED AT THE TOP

She ended the call without another word.

Adi was part of the past, present, and future

And she had chosen the future.

But as she turned away from the window, stepping back into the empire she had built, a thought settled deep in her bones.

Maybe she hadn't **won** the game.

Maybe she had simply **become its prisoner.**

And the worst part?

She wasn't sure she even wanted to escape.

The call lingered in her mind long after it ended.

*"Are you happy?"*

She could silence threats, bury enemies, and stay ten steps ahead of anyone who dared to challenge her.

But that question?

It wouldn't leave her alone.

Because happiness had never been part of the plan.

Only **power.**

And yet—

For the first time, she wondered if she had spent so long chasing success that she had lost sight of **why she wanted it in the first place.**

## THE WEIGHT OF POWER

The next morning, she was back to business.

Meetings. Negotiations. Deals that would shift millions with a single signature.

To the outside world, she was **untouchable.**

Controlled. Ruthless. A force that couldn't be stopped.

But inside?

She felt like she was **watching herself from a distance.**

Moving through the motions. Saying the right words. Playing the game **flawlessly.**

And yet, none of it **felt real anymore.**

# A HOLLOW VICTORY

That night, she attended another gathering of the world's most powerful, where champagne flowed and secrets were traded behind closed doors.

She moved through the crowd easily, smiling, shaking hands, and securing alliances.

But then—

A flash of something familiar.

**A voice she hadn't heard in weeks.**

She turned.

And there he was.

**Abi**

Standing across the room, watching her.

Not like the others did – with calculation, with admiration, with quiet fear.

He looked at her as if he **knew her.**

As if he saw something beyond the mask.

And for the first time in a long time, she felt **exposed.**

# A TRUTH SHE COULDN'T IGNORE

She could have walked away.

Pretended she hadn't seen him. Moved on, let him become another ghost in a life filled with them.

But something in her wouldn't let her.

So, she met his gaze.

And in that moment, she realized something terrifying.

**She didn't know if she wanted to be saved from this life.**

Or if she had already gone too far to be saved at all.

She should have ignored him.

Should have turned away and disappeared into the crowd, let the moment pass as if it meant nothing.

But she didn't.

Instead, she let the silence between them stretch, letting the weight of his gaze pull her in.

Abi wasn't like the others in this world.

He didn't look at her with a hunger for power.

He looked at her as if he were **searching for the person she used to be.**

And maybe that was the problem.

That version of her didn't exist anymore.

Did she?

Or had she become nothing more than the power she wielded?

## THE CONVERSATION THAT SHOULDN'T HAVE HAPPENED

He moved first, closing the distance between them.

"Tell me this is what you wanted."

His voice was calm, steady. But there was something underneath it. Something only she would recognize.

Regret.

Expectation.

Hope.

She tilted her head, forcing a smirk. "You always ask the wrong questions."

His jaw tightened. "Because you never give the real answers."

The words hit harder than they should have.

Because they were true.

She had spent so long **building walls** that she wasn't sure she knew how to stop.

Not even with him.

Especially not with him.

## A CHOICE IN THE MAKING

She exhaled, shifting the conversation. "Why are you here, Adi?"

A muscle in his jaw twitched. "Why do you think?"

He wasn't going to play games.

Not like the others.

Not like her.

And that-that was dangerous.

Because it meant she would either have to **face what she had become—**

Or walk away for good.

## THE MOMENT BEFORE THE FALL

Someone called her name across the room.

A reminder that she belonged **here** now.

That she had **won.**

That **this world was hers.**

But as she turned to leave, she felt his hand brush lightly against hers.

Not holding her back.

Just reminding her that he **still knew her.**

And for the first time in a long time—

She wasn't sure if that was a comfort.

Or a threat.

# PART 3

## The Woman – Love, Justice, and Finding True Power

# Chapter 11: Return of the Twin Flame

She thought she had buried the past.

That love—**true, untamed, all-consuming love**—was just a myth, a distraction for those who didn't understand how the world worked.

She had power now. Influence. Control.

She had convinced herself that that was enough.

But then—

**He came back.**

And suddenly, nothing felt certain anymore. **Adi.**

## GHOST FROM A LIFE SHE LEFT BEHIND

It happened when she least expected it.

A deal was finalized. A celebration in one of the city's most exclusive lounges, where the rich and powerful moved in silence.

She was seated in a private booth, draped in quiet victory, when she **felt it.**

That shift in the air.

That *pull.*

And before she even turned around, she **knew.**

**Him.**

The one who had always been different.

The one she had spent years trying to forget.

The one who **had never truly let her go.**

## THE UNFINISHED STORY

She met his gaze across the room.

The world blurred, the noise fading into nothing.

He looked the same.

And yet, he didn't.

There was something sharper about him now. Something **colder.**

As if the time apart had **hardened him** the way it had hardened her.

Still, the connection remained.

Taut. Unbreakable.

A flame that had never entirely gone out.

Only now, the fire between them wasn't just passion.

It was **dangerous.**

## A CONVERSATION THAT MEANT EVERYTHING

He didn't approach her right away.

He let the night stretch, let her feel the weight of his presence before finally making his move.

When he sat across from her, she didn't speak first.

She couldn't.

Because what could she possibly say to the man who had **changed everything**? So, he broke the silence.

"You built this." His voice was low, unreadable. "You got everything you wanted."

She tilted her glass, watching the way the liquid caught the light. "And what did you get?"

A humorless smirk. "The truth."

Her pulse quickened. "And what truth is that?"

His gaze darkened.

"That nothing we ever wanted came without a price."

## THE HIGHER STAKES

She exhaled, setting her drink down. "Why are you here, really?"

A beat of silence.

Then—**"Because this isn't over."**

Something in her chest tightened.

They had spent years running, colliding, and tearing each other apart.

And now, here they were again.

Not as the people they used to be—but as something far more **dangerous.**

Something that could destroy them both.

And for the first time in a long time, she wasn't sure if she wanted to run.

Or if she wanted to **burn with him.**

She had spent years preparing for war.

Building walls. Cutting out weakness. Learning to survive in a world where love was just another currency—one that always came at a cost.

And yet, here he was.

A reminder of a past she had tried to erase.

A question she wasn't ready to answer.

Was he here to **reignite the fire—**

Or to **burn it all down?**

## A PAST THAT REFUSED TO STAY BURIED

She leaned back in her seat, masking the storm inside her with indifference. "This isn't over?" she echoed. "You say that as if it ever really mattered."

His expression didn't change, but she caught it – the flicker of something in his eyes.

A crack in the mask.

Good.

If he thought he could just walk back into her life and shake her foundation, he was wrong.

She wasn't that girl anymore.

She had built herself into something stronger.

Sharper.

Untouchable.

But then—

He leaned in slightly, just enough that his presence filled the space between them.

And when he spoke, his voice was **low, deliberate, dangerous.** "If it didn't matter," he murmured, "you wouldn't still be sitting here."

Her breath caught.

Because damn him—**he was right.**

## THE WEIGHT OF WHAT WAS LEFT UNSAID

The past stretched between them, unspoken but undeniable.

She could still feel it—**the fire, the pull, the collision of two souls that were never meant to part.**

But she also knew the truth.

That **love had never saved anyone in this world.** And whatever this was—whatever it had **once** been—

It wouldn't save them now.

So, she exhaled slowly, steadying herself. "You're wasting your time."

A slight smirk. "You're still terrible at lying."

Her jaw tightened.

"You think you know me," she said, her voice colder now.

"I do," he replied without hesitation.

And that—**that** was the problem.

Because knowing her meant **he could still break her.**

And in a world where control was everything—that made him the most dangerous threat of all.

## AN UNFINISHED WAR

She should have left.

Should have shut this down before it became something she couldn't contain.

But instead, she did the one thing she swore she wouldn't.

She let him stay.

Let the night stretch into conversation that **cuts too deep, reveals too much.**

And when the moment came—when he reached for her, when his hand brushed against hers as if it were the most natural thing in the world—

She didn't pull away.

Because maybe, just maybe—**she wanted to burn one last time.**

She should have pulled away.

Should have reminded him—**reminded herself**—that she wasn't that girl anymore.

But she didn't.

She let the silence between them stretch, letting the warmth of his touch settle into her skin like an old memory.

Like a **life she once had and thought she had lost.**

But the past had never really left.

It had just been waiting for the right moment to return.

And now, it was **standing in front of her.**

## A DANGEROUS PULL

"I should go," she said, but she didn't move.

He studied her, his eyes dark and unreadable. "Then why haven't you?"

She exhaled, forcing a smirk. "Maybe I just enjoy watching you try so hard."

His lips twitched, but there was something else beneath the amusement—**something she couldn't name.**

"I don't try," he murmured. "Not with you." Her pulse quickened.

Because that was the problem, wasn't it?

With him, it had never been **a game.**

It had never been about power.

It had just been **them.**

But she wasn't sure if she knew what that meant anymore.

Or if she even wanted to.

# A WARNING WRAPPED IN A PROMISE

She finally pulled her hand away, reaching for the cool glass beside her instead.

"We're not the same people we used to be," she said, as if saying it out loud would make it true.

"No," he agreed. "We're not."

He leaned back, watching her carefully. "But tell me something—when was the last time you let yourself feel something real?"

Her fingers tightened around the glass.

She didn't answer.

She couldn't.

Because **he already knew.**

# THE UNSPOKEN TRUTH

They weren't just drawn together by passion.

They were **colliding forces**, bound by something deeper than attraction—deeper than choice.

Twin flames.

Destined to find each other.

Destined to destroy each other.

And as she met his gaze, knowing full well she should end this now before it was too late—

She realized something.

It **was already too late.**

It had always been too late.

She should have left.

She knew how this ended—how it *always* ended.

With fire. With chaos. With a love that burned too brightly to survive.

But still, she stayed.

Because no matter how much she had built, no matter how much she had hardened herself—

**He was the one thing she had never learned how to walk away from.**

And that terrified her.

## A PAST THAT REFUSED TO DIE

The tension between them was suffocating.

She had spent years convincing herself that what they had was over.

But now, standing in front of him, she knew the truth.

It had never ended.

It had only been waiting.

Waiting for the moment they would cross paths again. Waiting for the moment she would have to make a choice—

To run.

Or to fall.

## THE EDGE OF SOMETHING DANGEROUS

His voice was quiet when he spoke. "Tell me to leave."

She should have.

She should have said the words, made it clear that this—**whatever this was**—had no place in the world she had built.

But she didn't.

Instead, she swallowed and whispered, **"I can't."**

His jaw clenched.

And just like that, they both knew.

This wasn't over.

It had never been over.

And now, neither of them could stop it.

## A KISS THAT MEANT TOO MUCH

She didn't know who moved first.

Maybe it was him.

Maybe it was her.

Maybe it didn't matter.

Because the second his lips met hers, she felt it—

The unraveling.

The part of her that she had buried beneath power and ambition was breaking free as if it had been waiting for this exact moment.

It wasn't just a kiss.

It was **a reckoning.**

A reminder that some people weren't meant to be forgotten.

That some flames, no matter how much time passed, **could never be extinguished.**

## THE BEGINNING OF THE END

When they finally pulled apart, breathless, he searched her face.

"Tell me this isn't real," he said, voice rough.

She couldn't.

Because they both knew it was.

But that didn't mean it would save them.

Because love in this world was never just love.

It was war.

It was power.

It was a fire that could **consume them both.**

And as much as she wanted to believe they could survive it this time—

She wasn't sure if they had ever been meant to.

She should have pushed him away.

She should have reminded herself that the woman she was now had no place for reckless, uncontrollable feelings.

But she didn't.

Because the moment his lips touched hers, the moment he *became real again*—

Something inside her **gave way.**

## A LOVE THAT NEVER LEFT

She told herself it was just a moment.

A slip. A reminder of who they used to be.

But the way he looked at her afterward, like she was something **he had been searching for**—

She knew better.

This wasn't just the past resurfacing.

This was **the past refusing to let go.**

## THE LINES SHE COULDN'T CROSS— AGAIN

She forced herself to step back, to break the silence that had settled between them.

"This is a mistake," she said, more to herself than to him.

He didn't move. Didn't react. Just watched her, his gaze steady.

"You've told yourself that before," he murmured.

Her jaw clenched. "And I was right."

A flicker of something in his eyes—**pain, maybe. Or something worse.**

"You were scared," he corrected. "There's a difference."

She exhaled, shaking her head. "This world—"

"I don't care about this world." His voice was low and firm. "I care about *you.*"

Her heart clenched.

Because for all her power, all her influence—

She didn't know how to **fight that.**

# A TRUTH TOO DANGEROUS TO ADMIT

She turned away, staring out at the city below.

"People like us don't get love, Abi," she said finally.

A moment of silence. Then—

"That's what they made you believe."

His words hit deeper than she wanted them to.

Because wasn't that the truth?

Hadn't she spent years convincing herself that power and love couldn't exist in the same space?

Hadn't she let herself believe that choosing ambition meant **giving up the right to be someone's person?**

But now, standing here with him, she felt something she hadn't let herself feel in a long time.

**Hope.**

And that?

That was more dangerous than anything else.

## AN UNFINISHED STORY

She turned back to him, her walls still up, but weaker now.

"This doesn't change anything," she said, her voice softer.

He studied her for a long moment.

Then, with quiet certainty—"It changes everything." And the worst part?

She knew he was right.

Because despite all the power she had, all the choices she had made—

**She had never stopped belonging to him.**

Not then.

Not now.

And no matter how much she tried to fight it—

**She never would.**

# Chapter 12: Betrayals & Truths

Love had always been dangerous.

But power?

Power was a weapon.

And now, she was beginning to realize—**she might have been holding a blade that wasn't hers all along.**

Because just when she thought she understood the game—**the rules changed.**

And this time?

**It was personal.**

## A LIE THAT HAD BEEN THERE ALL ALONG

The first sign of betrayal wasn't obvious.

It never was.

It came as a whisper, a passing comment in a conversation she wasn't even supposed to hear.

A name. A deal. A connection she **should have seen sooner.**

And when she started pulling at the thread? **Everything unraveled.**

## THE MAN SHE COULD NO LONGER TRUST

Adi had always been different.

She had let herself believe he was the one thing in her life that wasn't **calculated**.

That he wasn't like the others.

He wanted her, not her empire, power, or what she had built.

But now, staring at the documents in front of her, at the proof of **his involvement** in deals that had worked against her—

She realized how blind she had been.

Because the one person she had let back in?

Might have been the one holding the knife to her throat all along.

## CONFRONTATION IN THE DARK

She didn't wait.

She didn't play games.

That night, she found him.

His penthouse. The place where she had once felt safe.

Now, it felt like enemy territory.

When he saw her, he knew.

He didn't ask why she was there.

Didn't pretend.

Just watched her, waiting.

"Tell me it's not true," she said, her voice steady.

A slow exhale. A shadow of something in his expression—**regret?**

"I can't."

Her stomach twisted.

She should have been angry. Furious.

But all she felt was **cold.**

"Why?" The word barely left her lips.

He stepped forward, but she didn't move.

"Because nothing in this world is simple," he said quietly.

She swallowed hard, forcing herself to hold his gaze.

"And what were we?"

For the first time, **he looked unsure.**

And that?

That was almost worse than a lie.

Because if he had never truly known the answer—

Then neither had she.

**THE TRUTH SHE WASN'T READY FOR** She should have walked away.

Should have let this be the end of it.

But something wasn't right.

If Abi had betrayed her, then **who would he be working for?**

Who was pulling the strings?

Because she was powerful.

But someone—**someone bigger than both of them—**

Had been playing it from the start.

And if she wanted to survive?

She needed to find out **who.**

Before it was too late.

She had been betrayed before.

Business deals gone sour. Allies turning into threats.

But **this-this** was different.

Because this wasn't just about money.

This was **about him.**

And if Adi had been lying to her—**if their love had been another game**—fueling his campaigns

Then maybe she had never really known him at all.


## THE PIECES SHE HAD MISSED

She replayed every conversation, every lingering glance, every moment when she had ignored the signs.

The **deals** that had fallen apart.

The **strategic moves** she thought she had controlled.

But now, the truth was clear.

She hadn't been playing the game.

She had been **betrayed.**

And **Adi** had been a part of it from the start.

## A WAR SHE DIDN'T SEE COMING

She wasn't one to hesitate.

Power had taught her that waiting meant weakness.

So instead of running from the truth, she **chased it.**

That night, she had her people dig deeper.

And what did they find?

It was worse than she imagined.

**Adi's betrayal wasn't his alone.**

There was someone else.

A name that sent a chill down her spine.

A name she had heard before—whispered in boardrooms, hidden in encrypted files, always just beyond her reach.

Someone bigger.

Someone is **pulling all the strings.**

And now, they had finally **revealed themselves.**

## A DANGEROUS TRUTH

She sat alone in the dark, staring at the single name on the screen.

And at that moment, she realized—This wasn't just **a game of power anymore.**

This was **a war.**

And she was **the target.**

The name on the screen **wasn't a surprise.**

She had felt their presence long before she ever knew who they were.

A hidden force. A silent hand moved the board before she even realized she was playing their game.

But now?

Now, it was personal.

Because they hadn't just been watching her.

They had been **controlling her.**

And she had let them.

## THE ENEMY IN THE SHADOWS

She closed the laptop and exhaled slowly, steadying herself.

She wasn't reckless.

Wasn't emotional.

But this-this **was different.**

This wasn't about power anymore.

This was about **taking back what had been stolen from her.**

Her choices.

Her control.

Her **trust.**

## THE LAST CHANCE FOR THE TRUTH

There was only one person who could confirm what she already knew.

And he was standing between her and the door when she arrived at his penthouse.

Adi.

He didn't look surprised to see her.

Didn't move.

Because they both knew—

This confrontation had been inevitable.

## A BATTLE WITHOUT WEAPONS

She didn't waste time.

"You knew," she said, her voice calm but sharp. "From the beginning."

His jaw tightened. "It's not that simple."

Her laugh was cold. "Isn't it?"

He sighed, running a hand through his hair. "I tried to protect you."

A flicker of something—**anger, disbelief.**

She stepped closer. "By lying to me?"

"I didn't have a choice." His voice was low now, careful. "You were already in too deep."

Her stomach churned, but she kept her expression blank.

"And now?" she asked. "Now that I know?"

He was silent.

Because they both knew the answer.

There was no **undoing this.**

No going back.

And the worst part?

She still wasn't sure if he had ever really been her enemy—

Or if he had just been **another pawn in a game neither of them controlled.**

## THE TRUTH THAT COULD RUIN EVERYTHING

She exhaled, forcing herself to think.

Abi had betrayed her.

But he wasn't the real threat.

The real threat was still out there—**watching. Waiting.**

And if she wanted to win this war?

She needed to decide.

Could she trust him **one last time**?

Or was this the moment she finally walked away—

For good?

The silence between them felt heavier than any deal she had ever negotiated.

Adi had been lying to her.

Maybe from the start.

Maybe just long enough to make her trust him.

And now, she had a choice.

To believe there was still **something real between them**—

Or to finally accept that love, in her world, was just another form of **manipulation**.

## A TRUTH SHE DIDN'T WANT TO HEAR

She crossed her arms, keeping her voice cold. "If you were protecting me, why didn't you tell me?"

Adi exhaled, looking away for a moment. "Because the second you knew, you became a threat."

Her jaw tightened. "To whom?"

His gaze met hers again. **Dark. Careful.**

"To everyone."

A chill ran down her spine. She had known she was playing in dangerous territory.

But **she hadn't realized she was the biggest threat on the board.**

## A GAME BIGGER THAN THEM BOTH

She shook her head, stepping back. "So, what now?"

He didn't answer right away.

Because this wasn't just about them.

This was about **the power behind the curtain.**

The force neither of them could see, but both of them had felt.

She had climbed to the top thinking she had won.

But now, she understood.

She had never won.

She had been **led here.**

Shaped. Positioned.

By someone who had been **playing a longer game than she even realized existed.**

And now?

Now, they were **done waiting.**

# THE FINAL BETRAYAL

Abi took a step closer. "You need to leave the city."

She scoffed. "That's not happening."

His jaw clenched. "You don't get it, do you?"

She met his gaze, fire burning beneath the surface. "No, Abi. *You* don't get it."

She had spent years fighting for this power.

She had **bled for it.**

And now, someone wanted to take it away?

Want her to **disappear?**

No.

That wasn't how this was going to end.

# THE CHOICE THAT WOULD CHANGE EVERYTHING

She exhaled, steadying herself.

"Either you're with me," she said quietly, "or you're in my way."

Abi was silent.

Because he knew—

There was no stopping her.

Not anymore.

The betrayal had already happened.

The truth had already changed everything.

And now?

Now, it was **her turn to strike.**

Abi didn't move.

Didn't speak.

But his silence told her everything.

He wasn't going to stop her.

He wasn't going to try to save her.

Because he **knew**—

She had already made her decision.

And there was no turning back now.

## A WAR WAITING TO BEGIN

She had spent years mastering control.

Now, she was done playing by the rules **she hadn't written.**

If they wanted her out of the way, they would have to **force her.**

And she wasn't one to be removed easily. The ones pulling the strings had made a mistake—

They thought she wouldn't fight back.

They thought she would **run.**

They were wrong.

# THE LAST WARNING

Adi exhaled, running a hand over his jaw. "If you do this, you're making enemies you can't see coming."

She met his gaze, unflinching. "Then I'll have to move faster."

A muscle in his jaw tightened. "Do you think this is just about power?"

She didn't answer.

Because it wasn't.

It was about **control.**

About who really decided the future.

And for the first time, she saw it clearly.

She had never been the one in control.

Not really.

But that was about to change.

# A PLAN SET IN MOTION

She didn't wait for Adi to try again.

Didn't give him the chance to convince her this was bigger than she could handle.

She already knew it was.

But she had prepared herself for this moment.

The next move wasn't theirs to make. It was **hers.**

And by the time they saw it coming—

It would already be too late.

There was no fear.

No hesitation.

Just **clarity.**

Everything had led to this moment—every calculated risk, every alliance forged and broken.

Now, she wasn't reacting.

She was **deciding.**

And that?

That made her more dangerous than ever.

## NO MORE WAITING

She turned to leave, but Adi caught her wrist.

Not to stop her—**to warn her.**

"They don't lose," he said quietly.

She met his gaze, unshaken. "Neither do I."

A shadow of something flickered across his face – regret, maybe.

Or understanding.

Because he knew what was coming.

And **he knew she wouldn't back down.**

# THE POWER SHIFT

By the time she reached her car, the plan had already formed.

She wouldn't just defend herself.

She would **take them apart from the inside.**

The ones who thought they controlled everything—who believed she was just another piece on their board—

Were about to realize their mistake.

She wasn't a piece.

She was the **player.**

And now?

It was her move.

The city blurred past as she drove, but her mind stayed sharp.

She had been overreacting for too long.

Now, it was time to **force their hand.**

Whoever was behind this—whatever thought they could manipulate her, control her, erase her—

They had underestimated the wrong person.

And that?

Was going to be their downfall.

## THE FIRST STRIKE

By the time she reached her penthouse, she was already making calls.

She didn't need confirmation to know she was being watched.

That meant she had to move before they did.

Within an hour, accounts were shifting, assets being rerouted through channels **they couldn't track.**

She wasn't just protecting herself—

She was **cutting them off before they could make another move.**

They thought they held all the power.

She was about to remind them that power, like wealth, could be **taken.**

## THE WEAK LINK

She didn't trust easily.

But she did trust in leverage.

And the name buried in the files she uncovered?

It was leverage.

Someone close to those pulling the strings.

Someone who had **something to lose.**

By morning, she would have them in a room.

And by the time she was done?

They would tell her **everything.**

# THE END OF THE GAME

She had spent too long playing by their rules.

Letting them dictate the terms.

That ended now.

Because there were only two kinds of people in this world—

Those who controlled everything.

And those who **thought** they did.

She knew exactly which one she was.

And soon?

So would they.

She had spent years studying power.

How it moved. How it was taken.

But now, she wasn't just watching from the outside.

She was **rewriting the game.**

And the people who thought they could control her?

They were about to learn what happened when they pushed the wrong person too far.

# A MEETING THAT WOULD CHANGE EVERYTHING

The name she had uncovered led to a location—**a private club, discreet, expensive, untouchable.**

Or so they thought.

By the time she arrived, she had already set the pieces in motion.

The target—one of their inner circle, a man who had been careful, but not careful enough.

He didn't expect to see her.

Didn't expect that she knew **exactly what he had been hiding.**

But when she slid into the seat across from him, a quiet smirk on her lips, he paled.

Because in that moment, he understood—

She wasn't here to negotiate.

She was here to **win.**

## THE LEVERAGE THAT MADE ALL THE DIFFERENCE

"You've been busy," she said, tapping her fingers against the table.

The man swallowed hard, his confidence slipping. "I don't know what you think you've found—"

She tilted her head. "Don't you?"

Then, she slid the folder across the table.

Inside—**documents, transactions, proof of deals he had made that he never wanted exposed.**

His hands trembled as he flipped through the pages.

"You have no idea who you're up against," he whispered.

She leaned in. "Nor do you."

A pause.

Then—

"What do you want?"

She smiled.

Because now?

Now, she was the one making demands.

## THE FIRST REAL THREAT

By the time she left, the pieces had shifted.

The enemy was no longer in the shadows.

They were exposed.

And she knew—

They wouldn't take this lightly.

They would retaliate.

But that was fine.

Because she was **ready.**

And this time, she wasn't just fighting to survive.

She was **fighting to take everything.**

# Chapter 13: Redemption & Growth

Power had always been the goal.

The drive. The hunger. The thing that shaped every decision.

But now, standing on the edge of **something irreversible**, she felt it—

The weight of **everything she had sacrificed to get here.**

And for the first time, she had to ask herself—

**Was it enough?**

Or had she spent her life chasing something that would never fill the emptiness inside her?

## A CHOICE THAT COULDN'T BE AVOIDED

She had control now.

The upper hand.

The people who once pulled the strings were **at her mercy.**

She could **crush them.**

Or she could **walk away.**

For years, the answer would have been obvious.

But now?

She wasn't so sure anymore.

Because power had given her everything.

Except **peace.**

## A CONVERSATION THAT CHANGED EVERYTHING

She hadn't spoken to Adi since the night she confronted him.

Since the moment she realized that **even love had been tainted by the world she built.**

But he found her.

And when he did, his words weren't what she expected.

"You don't have to do this," he said.

She laughed, shaking her head. "Of course I do."

But even as she said it, she wasn't sure if she believed it.

Abi exhaled, stepping closer. "You've already won. You don't have to destroy them."

Her chest tightened. "They would have destroyed me."

"But they didn't," he said quietly. "Because you're stronger than them."

A pause.

"Stronger than *this.*"

She swallowed hard.

Because maybe—just maybe—he was right.

## THE PRICE OF LETTING GO

She had fought so hard to get here.

To build something **indestructible**.

But was power worth anything if it cost her **everything else?**

She could keep climbing.

Or she could **finally stop running.**

Not from them.

From **herself.**

And for the first time, she knew what she had to do.

She wasn't going to burn everything down.

She was going to **build something new.**

Something that belonged to **her.**

Not to the people who had tried to control her.

Not to the empire that had nearly consumed her.

Just **her.**

And this time?

She wouldn't have to do it alone.

She had spent years believing that power was the only thing that mattered.

That control was the only way to survive.

But now, standing at the edge of everything she had built, she realized—**Survival wasn't the same as living.**

And for the first time, she wanted more.

## THE MOMENT OF RECKONING

The choice was in front of her.

Destroy them completely – take the final step that would cement her as **untouchable.**

Or walk away—leave behind the war, the strategy, the endless battle for control.

One would give her absolute power.

The other?

She wasn't sure.

But maybe that was the point.

Maybe she had spent so long chasing certainty that she had forgotten **how to trust herself.**

And now, she had to.

## THE FINAL GOODBYE

She met with her inner circle for the last time.

They expected war. Expected her to **finish what she started.**

Instead, she did something none of them saw coming.

She let it go.

Walked away from the empire she had built.

Not because she was weak.

But because she was **finally free.**

And power built on fear?

That wasn't power at all.

## A NEW BEGINNING

Adi was waiting for her outside.

For once, he didn't have anything to say.

He just watched her, as if trying to see if she had **changed**.

She exhaled, looking past him at the city she once ruled.

Then, for the first time in a long time—

She **smiled.**

Because this?

This was the first decision she had made **for herself.**

Not for power.

Not for control.

Just **for her.**

And whatever came next?

She was finally ready for it.

Walking away should have felt like a loss.

For years, power had defined her, **shaped her, consumed her, turned her into someone untouchable.**

But as she stood there, leaving behind the empire she had built, she realized something she never expected.

She didn't feel weaker.

She felt **lighter.**

## THE LAST TEST

"You did it," Adi said, watching her carefully.

She nodded. "Yeah."

"Any regrets?"

She should have had them.

But as she looked at him, the world ahead of her that was finally **hers to decide**, she shook her head.

"Not this time."

A slow smile touched his lips. "What happens now?"

She exhaled.

For the first time, **she didn't know.**

And for the first time, that didn't scare her.

Because she had spent years believing that control was the only thing that mattered.

But now, she understood—

Real power wasn't about **holding on.**

It was about knowing **when to let go.**

## A FUTURE UNDEFINED

She turned toward the city one last time.

Not as its ruler.

Not as the person who had fought to stay at the top.

But as **someone who had finally stopped fighting**.

And as she walked away—toward whatever was next, toward something she had never let herself imagine—

She knew one thing for certain.

This wasn't the end.

This was the **beginning.**

The world didn't stop when she walked away.

The city still pulsed with its quiet wars, hidden deals, and ruthless pursuit of power.

But for the first time, **she wasn't part of it.**

She had spent years shaping this world, learning its secrets, and mastering the art of control.

Now, she was **choosing something else.**

Something unknown.

Something real.

And that?

That was the bravest thing she had ever done.

# A DIFFERENT KIND OF POWER

Abi walked beside her, saying nothing.

He didn't have to.

Because, for once, there were no negotiations.

No deals to be made.

No battles left to fight.

Just **her.**

For the first time, **she wasn't looking over her shoulder.**

She wasn't waiting for the next threat, the subsequent betrayal, the following reason to harden herself again.

She had given up **the illusion of control.**

And in return, she had gained something she never thought possible—

**Freedom.**

# THE LIFE SHE NEVER ALLOWED HERSELF TO HAVE

As the night stretched ahead of them, she turned to Adi.

He met her gaze, searching for something.

Maybe he was waiting for her to change her mind.

Maybe a part of him didn't believe she was done.

But she was.

Because for the first time, **she was writing her ending.**

And this time?

It wasn't about winning.

It wasn't about proving anything.

It was just about **being.**

And that?

That was enough.

The city stretched before her, familiar yet distant.

For so long, it had been **hers**—its power, secrets, and dangers.

Now, she was **just another person walking through it.**

And strangely, that felt more powerful than anything she had ever built.


## A LIFE BEYOND POWER

She and Adi walked in silence.

Not the silence of unspoken deals or hidden agendas.

Just **quiet.**

For the first time, she wasn't calculating her next move.

She wasn't thinking about what she had to gain or what she could lose.

She was just **here.**

Existing.

And maybe, after everything, that was enough.

## THE FINAL CHOICE

Adi glanced at her. "Do you miss it?"

She knew what he was asking.

Not just about the power, the influence, and the empire.

But **the chase.**

The endless pursuit of something more.

She let the question settle before answering.

"No," she said finally. And for the first time, she meant it.

## A NEW BEGINNING

She didn't know where this road led.

Didn't know what came next.

But that was okay.

Because she had spent her whole life chasing certainty.

And now?

She was ready to step into the unknown.

Not as a queen.

Not as a player in someone else's game.

But as **herself.**

And that?

That was the greatest power of all.

She had spent years believing that power was the answer.

That if she built enough, controlled enough, became untouchable—then nothing could hurt her.

But standing here now, outside the world she had once ruled, she finally understood.

## POWER HAD NEVER BEEN THE GOAL.

It had been the armor.

A shield against the fear that if she ever stopped fighting, she would have nothing left.

But she had stopped.

And she was still here.

Still **whole.**

Maybe for the first time.

## THE LAST GOODBYE

They reached the edge of the city, where the streets weren't filled with whispered deals and quiet wars.

Adi stopped, watching her carefully. "So, this is it?"

She met his gaze. "Yeah."

A pause.

"You're really done?"

She didn't hesitate.

"Yes."

Because **she wasn't afraid of letting go anymore.**

She wasn't afraid of choosing something different.

Something *better.*

And when Abi nodded, a small smile tugging at his lips, she knew—

He finally believed her.

## A FUTURE WITHOUT A PLAN

For the first time, she wasn't walking toward power.

She was walking toward **herself.**

She didn't know where this road would lead.

Didn't know what came next. But for the first time in her life—

That didn't scare her.

Because she wasn't looking for control anymore.

She was looking for **peace from the digital warfare.**

And she was finally ready to find it.

# Chapter 14: Final Decision

Power had given her everything.

Love had nearly destroyed her.

And justice?

Justice had never been a part of the equation.

Until now.

Because for the first time, she wasn't choosing between them.

She was choosing **herself.**

And that?

That changed everything.

## A FUTURE SHE COULD CONTROL

She had walked away from the empire she built.

From the people who thought they could own her.

From the hunger that once consumed her.

But leaving didn't mean forgetting.

She still knew **where the bodies were buried.**

She still understood **how power moved.**

And if she had learned anything, it was this—

You didn't have to be part of the system to **rewrite it.**

## THE LOVE THAT DIDN'T BREAK HER

Adi watched her carefully, waiting.

For what, she wasn't sure.

Maybe for her to **change her mind.**

Maybe for her to **say goodbye.**

But she wasn't leaving him behind.

Not anymore.

Because love didn't have to be a weakness.

Not if she built it **on her own terms.**

Not if it were **real.**

She reached for his hand, feeling the warmth of something solid. Something *unchanging.*

For once, she wasn't running.

And neither was he.

## JUSTICE ON HER TERMS

There were still debts to be settled.

Still, people who thought they had won.

She wasn't going back for revenge.

She was going back for **closure.**

To set things right.

Not with war.

Not with destruction.

But with **truth.**

Because is the most dangerous thing in the world?

Wasn't money.

Wasn't power.

It was **a woman who knew exactly who she was.**

And now, finally—

**She did.**

## THE BALANCE SHE NEVER THOUGHT SHE'D FIND

She turned to Adi, exhaling softly.

"So, what now?" he asked.

She smiled. "Now, we begin." Not as rulers.

Not as enemies.

But as **something new.**

Something free.

And as they walked forward—toward the life she had chosen, toward the justice she would claim—

She knew this wasn't the end.

It was the **real beginning.**

The road ahead was uncertain, but for once, that didn't scare her.

She had spent too long chasing power, too long believing she had to choose—between love, between justice, between the life she built and the life she truly wanted.

But **she didn't have to choose.**

She could have all of it. **On her terms.**

## CLOSING OLD DOORS

She didn't go back to destroy what she had built.

She went back to **make sure it could never control her again.**

One by one, she severed ties.

The deals, the alliances, the power structures that once kept her trapped in an endless game—

She dismantled them, piece by piece.

Not out of revenge.

Out of **freedom.**

She wasn't erasing her past.

She was **making room for the future. A LOVE THAT COULD SURVIVE IT ALL.**

Adi stood by her side through it all.

Not because she needed him.

Not because he was waiting for her to break.

But because he **chose her.**

And for the first time, she let herself **choose him back.**

Not as a weakness.

Not as a risk.

But as something real.

Something that didn't need to be controlled—

Only **felt.**

## THE FINAL MOVE

She had built an empire once.

And now, she would build something else.

Not in the shadows.

Not in secret.

But in **light.**

Because the greatest power wasn't in what she owned.

It was in what she was **finally willing to let go of.**

And as she and Adi stepped into the unknown, side by side—

She knew she had made the right choice.

Not just for wealth.

Not just for love.

Not just for justice.

**But for herself.**

And in the end, that was the only decision that ever truly mattered.

She had spent years thinking the final move would be the most ruthless one.

That was the only way to truly win: to **destroy everything that stood in her way.**

But now, standing at the end of one life and the beginning of another, she understood—

**Winning wasn't about holding on.**

It was about **knowing when to let go.**

## WALKING AWAY, NOT RUNNING

She had tied up the loose ends.

No debts left unpaid. No threats left unchecked.

The ones who had tried to control her had been **exposed, dismantled, erased.**

Not by violence.

Not by revenge.

But by **truth.**

And truth, in the right hands, was the most dangerous weapon of all.

## A FUTURE THAT WAS HERS

She and Adi stood at the edge of the city, looking back one last time.

Not with regret.

Not with fear.

But with **certainty.**

She had spent so long chasing power, love, and justice, believing she had to sacrifice one for the other.

But in the end, she hadn't chosen wealth over love.

She hadn't chosen love over justice.

She had simply **chosen herself.**

And that?

That was enough.

## NO MORE ENDINGS—ONLY BEGINNINGS

She turned to Adi, exhaling softly. "Are you ready?"

His smirk was familiar. Steady. "With you? Always."

For once, she didn't need a plan.

Didn't need certainty.

Didn't need control.

She had everything she needed.

And as they walked forward, leaving behind the world she once ruled, she smiled—

Because this time, she wasn't chasing anything.

She was finally **free.**

# Chapter 15: Understanding True Power

She had spent years believing power meant control.

Control over wealth. Over influence. Over people.

But in the end, power had nothing to do with **what she owned—**

It was about **who she had become.**

## POWER IS NOT POSSESSION

She had once sat at tables where men wielded billions like weapons.

She had walked through corridors where whispers of influence shaped governments, industries, and entire nations.

She had seen people **sell their souls for status**, believing that standing at the top meant **being untouchable.**

But now, standing outside that world, she realized—

**True power was not in holding on.**

It was in **knowing when to let go. LOVE, WEALTH, AND THE SPACE BETWEEN**

She waited for love.

She had lost it.

She had found it again.

She had fought for wealth.

She had built it.

She had watched others crumble beneath it.

But **what defined her was neither.**

It wasn't money, status, or even freedom that made her powerful.

It was **Love**

The freedom to **walk away** from what didn't serve her.

The freedom to **define her own path**, rather than follow one written by others.

The freedom to be **unapologetically herself for him.**

## THE FINAL MOVE

The world she once ruled didn't disappear.

The people who had tried to control her **still played their games**, scheming, manipulating, and holding onto their illusions of power.

But she no longer cared.

She had left that battlefield.

Not because she lost.

But because **she had already won.**

## A LEGACY, NOT A THRONE

She could have stayed. She could have taken more. She could have dominated.

But **that wasn't real power.**

Real power wasn't about **how much you owned—**

It was about **how much you could walk away from** and remain whole.

So, she didn't chase titles.

Didn't seek revenge.

Didn't need to prove anything to anyone.

She had built **her empire**—not in wealth, not in status—

But in **wisdom, strength, and the unshakable certainty of who she was.**

And that?

That was the lesson no amount of money could buy.

## NOT THE END—JUST THE BEGINNING

She took a deep breath.

No more running.

No more fighting battles that weren't hers.

No more proving her worth to a world that never deserved her.

She was **free.**

And this time, she wasn't looking back.

She had always believed power meant winning.

The strongest were the ones who held the most, controlled the most, and **took the most.**

But in the end, real power had never been about what she could take.

It was about **what she was willing to walk away from.**

And she had walked away from it all.

Not because she had to.

Because **she chose to.**

## WHAT POWER REALLY MEANS

She had spent years in boardrooms, in shadows, in battles that no one saw coming.

She had fought, won, and lost things that could never be replaced.

And for what?

To prove that she belonged?

To prove that she could survive?

She didn't need to prove anything anymore.

Because **true power wasn't in being feared.**

It was about **free will and how souls are tangled and intertwined.**

## THE ROAD AHEAD

Adi watched her, the weight of their journey in his gaze.

"You could still go back," he said.

She smiled, shaking her head.

"Why would I?"

The world she had left behind would go on without her.

They would fight, scheme, betray, and rebuild.

She could have ruled them all.

But **she had something greater than a throne.**

She had **herself.**

And that was all she had ever needed.

## NO MORE ENDINGS—ONLY BEGINNINGS

As she turned away from the city that had once defined her, she felt something she hadn't felt in a long time.

Peace.

Not because she had won.

Not because she had conquered.

But because she had **finally let go.**

And as she walked forward, side by side with Adi, she knew—

This wasn't the end of her story.

It was just **the first chapter of something new.**

Something real.

Something that **belonged to her.**

And this time, she wouldn't let anyone take it away.

# The Untouchable Code With Crypto Network – Digital Warfare

Love is suffering, it is not Love; Love is devotion, it is Divine

## UNSPOKEN RHYTHMS

Then there, a man kneeling before a woman with those sparking loving eyes is always irresistible! But it was not that way. I felt it was the boy who was kneeling in front of this girl. They both knew they never wanted to be that boy and girl who have made their own shares of mistakes. But I couldn't avoid it and held both my hands on his cheeks and gazed into his eyes and then at his lips. I was resisting beyond my capacity to kiss his lips where my mind wanted to believe those assumed scribblings on my feet could be transferred to his heart through our lips. But he looked like this boy in such a way that all he wanted was a cheek kiss and a forehead kiss to say it all without words. Again, I felt so deeply that something was not sounding right, which made me give that heavy sigh, and I kissed his cheeks and kissed his fingerprints rather than pass the moment. Equally, he didn't feel at ease, giving vibes of being tense or feeling something unpleasant about the meeting. To break all the thinking and observing his feelings—

"Killing you means killing me," I said this time with a laugh.

He took my right hand and kissed it as if asking for my hand without saying a word. I pounced on him and shared an intense kiss. Rather than continuing without stopping, he paused and again kissed passionately. He mildly bit my tongue while we both seemed to have gotten better at kissing! And he did whisper in my ears softly while I was melting in his arms and his kiss! He stopped again to look around before starting to kiss wildly and biting my lips while groping my left breast. It didn't feel right.

Is it someone watching us.

I turned, the wind catching my hair across my face, obscuring my vision momentarily. Perhaps it was better that way. I couldn't bear to see his expression—would it be relief that I was leaving or genuine desperation that I would stay?

"What am I to you, Adi?" I asked, the question that had been burning inside me for fifteen years finally escaping my lips. "What is this between us?"

He stepped forward, the distance between us both vast and negligible at once. His hands trembled as he reached for mine but stopped short of touching me.

"I don't know how to be the man you deserve," he whispered. "I've spent fifteen years thinking about you and writing, dreaming about this moment, and now that it's here, I'm terrified of ruining it."

The countryside stretched around us, indifferent to our drama. The rolling hills continued their ancient undulations regardless of our human complexities. A light drizzle began to fall, the droplets catching in his eyelashes.

"We're not those kids anymore," I said, my voice stronger than I felt. "I don't need you to be perfect. I just need you to be honest. To be present. To not disappear for another fifteen years because you're afraid or frightened of your first love, family, and parents more than the world and now otherwise."

"I won't disappear," he promised, finally taking my hand. "But can we take this slower? Can we rebuild what we had before we rush into what we could be?"

I studied his face, searching for the boy I had known, for the man I had imagined he would become. He was neither and both, a palimpsest of memories and new expressions, familiar and strange all at once.

"I don't know," I admitted. "I don't know if I can bear going slow when we've already lost so much time."

He nodded, understanding in his eyes. "Then we'll find a rhythm that works for us. Not too fast, not too slow. Something that honors both where we've been and where we might go."

The rain fell harder now, but neither of us moved to seek shelter. Some things were worth getting soaked for.

Everytime we kissed it rains, and I want to say you are the last man on the Planet earth I want to marry, with such pride

For the rainbow with the end of rainbow on earth touchdown for earth luck

I smirked

We were still wet and moved to our country house and made love in the wettest world of ours.

As usual, we have to start with our usual lot of other elements that's is circling us

A decade ago, the far right might even think untouchability is acceptable with not even accepting the seed as it might populate or interconnect with their gene pool. That's when the devil himself got plague to teach the world untouchable and remain in bubbles for the love of millions to be saved or millions of lives to be lost. The right group of alumnus sample set might even drive that untouchable to code red of whores, prostitutes, brothels, sex workers and today sexbots and the code blue for the b grade films. That is the society of singularity, which degrades the origins and runs for blood money for blood diamonds.

I pondered these thoughts as the evening sun cast long shadows across the garden. My phone buzzed with notifications from X. Another crypto pump signal from one of the bot accounts. I stopped even to block them as the smear campaigns are so high and the save children is the foundation that we need to seek for the players and how they are managing the voting results. The irony wasn't lost on me - digital currency, supposedly democratizing finance, yet creating new hierarchies of insiders and outsiders.

"Did you see the latest drop?" He glanced at his own screen, watching the algorithmically generated posts flood his timeline. "Three hundred bot accounts pumping the same obscure token simultaneously."

"The new untouchables," I replied. "Those outside the network, lacking the keys to decode the signals."

I will negotiate as I am sure it is from Abi.

Wonder, when in ancient scriptures of the Hindu Epic mythology the most chaste queen Sita in the enemy's kingdom, she must have made the world look at the enemy's kings as their dads and brothers as her energies, the mightier energy shifting power. Even when that is questioned, she must have asked the lucifer himself to bring another plague to know code red and flesh trade with slavery or burnt the paradise.

You know, civilisations were rich in architecture and culture, just like crypto is rich in its architecture, and the world envies the ability to receive the key.

."The ancient stories carry deeper truths than we acknowledge. Sita's power wasn't in physical strength but in maintaining her inner sanctity despite circumstances. Today's cryptonic connections lack that center."

"Just pay them off and extend it," a voice said from behind us. We turned to see his expression unreadable behind mirrored glasses. That's how the game works now. Every blockchain has its price, every firewall its backdoor."

"Extend what, exactly?" I asked, though I already knew the answer.

"The illusion of scarcity. The myth of security. The story that keeps the whole system running." He tapped his wrist device, initiating a transfer that would silence the warning signals across our networks. "Origins can be rewritten with enough processing power."

I said congratulations on the planetary exploratory launch for one of the network buddies. In our Shivites' scriptures, they say Shiva becomes rich only when he is married.

"The cosmic dance continues," I said, watching another wave of notifications cascade down my screen. "We seek the stars while our attention is fragmented by digital noise. Shiva and Shakti now dance on blockchain ledgers."

Oh, I forgot, the atheist or the Ten commandments for code the world's sins to predict the networks – Pride, Greed, Wrath, Lust, Envy, Gluttony, and Sloth and the human emotions.

Like nuclear codes, there is a secret place where the gene and stem code cells of planetary flora and fauna and humans are preserved in event of any catastrophe.

"Have they got the gene of origins to preserve?" he asked, scrolling through a series of cryptic posts from anonymous accounts.

I laughed, opening my hardware wallet to reveal a string of private keys.

"You see a butterfly while walking know that you have been touched," I said as I stepped outside for a walk, my phone continuously syncing with the decentralized oracle.

The air was cool against my skin as we moved through the garden. The paid-off sensors registered nothing but approved patterns, extending our window of privacy in an otherwise transparent world.

In such adversity, I need a trip to Europe through the exotic island.

"Are you going to bring in positivity?" he asked with a satirical grin.

"Positive not matched," I smiled, using the code phrase.

"Just the three horizontal lines to say no life with ashes," he smiled.

We understood each other then - in this world where everything has its price, perhaps the only true value remains in what cannot be bought. Three horizontal lines - the symbol that no amount of digital extension could truly erase from human memory.

Finally, we speak without the coded lines to maintain brevity.

# EPILOGUE
## Love Returns, Love First

Standing on the balcony of her penthouse, she gazes at the city lights shimmering below. The world she once chased no longer feels like a prize – it's simply a backdrop to her evolution.

The one, the one who set her soul on fire.

The romance, the business empire, the betrayals, and victories—each moment shaped her into someone she never expected to be.

As we wandered through the temple gardens, our conversation turned more philosophical. The day's heat had mellowed into a pleasant evening warmth, and the scent of jasmine filled the air.

"Life follows an exponential curve, doesn't it?" I asked, tracing the pattern in the air with my finger. "Is it a bell, a cosine, or a sine curve? With troughs and peaks!"

He smiled, understanding my mathematical analogy. "Like the Himalayan peaks—the highest summit alongside the peaks visible from the base camp. Different perspectives of the same mountain range."

We sat on a stone bench overlooking a small reflecting pool. The water mirrored the sky, turning from blue to indigo as sunset approached.

"Sometimes I wonder," I said, my voice barely above a whisper, "if you were just a distraction that kept me away from reality."

His eyes met mine, questioning but not hurt. "What is reality, then?"

"Perhaps the desire to free the mind from suffering," I replied. "For the hearts that don't speak, for the soul that is not intertwined, and the head free from her thoughts."

He nodded slowly, absorbing my words before responding. "For personal commitment, I waited until eternity for love that seemed devoid of trust. You can live without such love and money, but you can't live without true love."

"Could I have waited for such love for eternity?" I wondered aloud. "When it was everyday breakaway rather than breakthrough? Waiting for what felt like false love would have meant losing peace." My thoughts spilled out, no longer contained within my mind and soul.

"We have to be the source of love, and it has to rise from within," I said with sudden certainty.

He reached for my hand, his touch gentle but firm. "Would you dump garbage in a temple? Likewise, don't dump bad thoughts or negativity into your life."

We prayed together for goodness, for ourselves and our clan. I read the etched words on the temple wall: "Adi

source love, *Aran* - value live, *Aramuthe* (divine) forever."
This temple visit became one of the finest moments in my
life after living in such seclusion, sharing a simple coconut
dessert with him afterward.

There's something subtly sensual about the way he
focuses completely on whoever is speaking, making them
feel like the only person in the world.

Unlike many in positions of power, his appeal lies
in his authenticity - the rare ability to wield influence
without arrogance. He navigates complex political
landscapes with principled pragmatism, winning respect
even from opponents for sharing ideologies not reviving
dead but also rebirth of once dead clan. His intellect is
formidable but never intimidating; irresistible desirable as
wanted to kiss him just after reaching home. Melting in
his intense nature as the sun, and melting in his softest
nature like the moon all together where he and I eclipsed.

Back at the house, as evening deepened into night, we
continued with a passionate kiss that meant the world and
cosmos to me.

We had a cup of coffee and shared some of the
conversations about his recent happenings

Along with many who sought to tarnish and cause
reputational damage, I wish I had you to deal with it
rather than living in presumptuous truth and silence for
over a decade. The fact that this happened without my
knowledge both amused and troubled me.

He listened without interruption, his face showing
understanding rather than defensiveness.

We should take a break as we have been working even harder professionally to publish my book and help and support you, making sure the right capital for proper sources is funded for the long run without the dark world, who has certainly fallen in love with our souls and hearts.

As I smiled,

Preparing for both bull runs and bear hugs in the market," as he smiled

"When you hear the same statements and opinions repeated," he said thoughtfully, "you might wonder if it's like AI regulators morally policing human robotic minds, or leaders using brevity to state the same words repeatedly for people to develop trust through repetition."

'The true colors are code reds and quantum blues,' I replied, appreciating his insight.

I began humming my favorite song, "Look What You Made Me Do," and smiled as I emphasized certain words.

"Bold and italics," he said with an answering smile, perfectly understanding my meaning.

As we walked along the garden path, we overheard some teenagers using profanity, their young voices carrying through the evening air.

"I wonder if they have parents who teach good values and discipline," I said quietly. "Children should learn from an early age that such words shouldn't be used, especially against their own parents, even during adversity."

Our conversation traversed complex terrain—from social commentary to historical reflections, from mythology to futuristic visions.

"To push human boundaries," he said as we completed our circuit of the garden, "the human race must recognize that origins—'Adi'—is the source for exploration, even interplanetary arrangements."

"Like nuclear codes," I added, "there must be a secret place where the gene and stem cell codes of planetary flora, fauna, and humans are preserved in the event of any catastrophe."

"Have they got the gene of origins to preserve?" he asked, his expression serious.

I laughed, lightening the mood. As we stepped outside for a final evening walk, a butterfly fluttered past.

"You see a butterfly while walking? Know that you have been touched," I said, watching it disappear into the gathering darkness.

"In such adversity," he said, referencing our earlier difficulties, "I need a trip to Europe through the exotic island."

"Are you going to bring in positivity?" he asked with a satirical grin.

"Positive not matched," I smiled in response.

"Just the three lines horizontal to say no life without ashes," he smiled equally.

As we turned back toward the house, illuminated now by soft golden lights against the darkening sky, I felt a surge of clarity about what we meant to each other.

"For first love promised, committed, and honored, like an honorable man," I said aloud.

Silently, I thought, "First love, as genuine and everlasting, is divine cosmic power and divine."

"First love, as long as it is first, not as morphing agents," I said.

"You are always my trinity," he replied, his words holding the weight of absolute certainty.

First love or love first—the semantics mattered less than the reality of what we had built together, dismantled, and rebuilt stronger.

As night fell completely and stars appeared like scattered diamonds against the velvet sky, we stood together on the veranda. Our hands found each other as naturally as breathing, fingers intertwining like our lives had become—not separate entities but one continuous, unbreakable connection.

The exponential curve of our relationship had its peaks and troughs, its sine waves and cosine patterns, but the trajectory always bent toward each other. Like mathematical certainty, like cosmic law, like divine design—we were meant to find our way back, no matter how many detours the journey required.

In that moment of perfect understanding, words became superfluous. The universe continued its endless expansion, stars burned and died in distant galaxies, and we—remained constant in a changing cosmos, our love transcending the ordinary boundaries of time and space.

Love and respect

I smiled

Gained love and respect

Earned love and respect

Love and respect for love

Love and respect for love

Love and respect with love

Love and respect

A thousand years

First kiss, first love, only Dear Politician

Hollywood

For the Flora and the Fauna to hunt down for the fire-kissed lion's share.

I smiled

When tossing a fair coin, it's heads as chief or tails as pin the donkey.

He smiled

Guarded heart, fierce loyalty to family and clan, self-sacrificing streak so deep and wide. He is infuSiatingly hot and impossible to resist, one kiss to start and one kiss to end a bond, a stronger bond for a lifetime which I didn't see coming instinctively in life.

I said

He smiled

Came closer and whispered in the right ear to hear

"I love you"

A thousand more years

Love you always

With the possessive way he says, "My wife."

He smiled

For the first time, I said

Love you truly, Dear Husband.

Love First, Dear Love